To — Justin Sykes

14 Tales of Christmas

Neil A. Waring

Merry Christmas Neil

Old Trails Publishing

http://oldtrailspublishing.blogspot.com

Christmas can be any time of the year in the West.

Neil A. Waring

Old Trails Publishing
http://oldtrailspublishing.blogspot.com

This book is dedicated to my mom, born on Christmas day 1920. Now gone for more than a decade, our family will never celebrate a Christmas without thinking of her. She loved everything about Christmas and gave my wife and me that same attitude. Everything from Christmas paper to Christmas goodies, Christmas Carols, and Christmas lights, around our house, growing up, she was Christmas.

And a very special thanks to readers of western and historical fiction everywhere and to my wife Jan, once again, for her patience with this project as my first reader and listener, as she has been for all five of my books.

Contents

Note from the Author

I hope readers will feel blessed and entertained by these western tales of Christmas. Some are set in times long passed, some are modern, a few fall in the middle, but all are westerns through and through.

Enjoy & Merry Christmas

Neil

Christmas tales are for the young, or so it has been said. But these stories are for the young at heart, because the magic of Christmas can touch everyone, young and old.

~1~
A Wind River Christmas

The old mountain man was starving, but not for food. He needed to talk, talk to someone besides himself. By his recollection, it had been seven years, no eight, eight years since he had spoken a word to another human. Oh he talked, spoke to his horses, the trees and sometimes the wind. But did they listen, he wasn't sure. He lived high, so high that the Indians didn't come up, not this far into the Wind Rivers.

It was Christmas Eve, he knew it because he kept a calendar, Christmas Eve 1842. A loner his entire life he had taken to reading the *Bible* the past few years and to praying, he'd become a praying man. Tonight he prayed for another person to talk with. He'd never done that before, asked God for something. Instead, he said thankful prayers. He was happy, happy alone, happy in the high mountains, and not wanting for anything in life. Grateful that he had grown to a ripe old age, at least he was happy and thankful until a few days ago. Now he needed someone to talk with.

The snow fell gently on a windless night as he knelt in the cabin and asked for a friend, if only for a day. After his Amen, he knew it was pure folly. God would never answer such a trivial and self-serving prayer. But in the morning his life would change, change forever.

He dreamt of Christmas as a kid, even though his parents never celebrated it. He dreamed of happy times and slept, slept soundly. When he woke the sun was up and looked like it had been for more than an hour, maybe two. Ol' Ezra wasn't ready to get up, not yet. He rolled over and pulled the buffalo robes up under his chin. Sixty-six years that is what he was today, Christmas day. He counted once again in his mind, born in 1776, the year of the countries great birthday. He remembered years ago when the ol' was tagged in front of his name and he became ol' Ezra.

That was at the rendezvous on the Green in 1825. Someone told him the average life was less than 50 years. Ezra didn't know if it was true but if it was, he was quite old, turning 50 in less than a year, and most thankful.

Now more than a decade later he was thankful every day that he still could shoot, trap, walk, cook, and make meat with his hunting skills. Grateful every day, but he wished he had someone to talk with, he needed to talk. When he quit on the rendezvous, he quit people. The goings on at the rendezvous had become too wild for him, too wild for a mild mannered person who came west in 1818, an old man of 42 misspent years.

The 42 years were not actually wasted, but Ezra saw his life as idle and shiftless. Others didn't see it that way, he never missed work, not once in thirty years. He worked at storekeeping and bookkeeping and he was good at it. By his fortieth birthday, he had saved more money than most would make in a lifetime, but it didn't make him happy.

For happiness, he read and studied the classics. Most looked at him as an educated, but somewhat odd man. What they didn't know is that is the way he saw himself, educated but curious and he felt stuck, trapped in his job, stuck in his life. It wasn't like he couldn't leave, he had no family, none at all.

He married at 26, but his wife died the next year of phenomena. She was frail and unassuming, one who loved to read and to talk with her husband. She was gone now for 40 years and Ezra still missed her.

Ezra rolled on his side and pulled the robes up tight, one more time, thought better of it, pushed them off and got up for the day. Lacing up his moccasins Ezra still thought of his town life days. Seemed like such a long time ago when

he left New York City. Left the city and walked
in as straight a line as he could all the way to
the mountains in the west. The Wind River
Mountains, mountains Ezra was sure were
painted by the hand of God himself.

Twenty-four years ago he'd made that life-
changing decision and everything was perfect,
until now. Now he wanted someone to talk with,
if only for a day.

It had taken Ezra almost six years to build
the cabin, a cabin like none other. Four rooms
with a loft upstairs. Often he wondered why he
had been so elaborate with his living quarters.
Once he started building, he enjoyed it so much
he wasn't sure he ever wanted to finish. And
now, he liked the way it looked. A large common
room took up more than half the front of the
cabin. Off the back of the common room were
three equally spaced doors. A door to his
storeroom, a door to a corner room with stalls
for his horses if need be during cold and stormy
times. And his bedroom, small and dominated
by his massive hand hewn aspen log bed. The
loft was built for guests although he had never
entertained anyone, not a single guest.

In his years on the mountain, he had only
seen one other human being and that was only
once. An Indian and only a glimpse, looked like

4

a young boy, one between childhood and warrior status. When Ezra never again saw him he assumed he was on a vision quest and most likely did not see the old mountain man through the darkness of the high country forest.

Ezra walked outside, to the front porch wood pile. He breathed the mountain air, he loved that, first of the day, outside deep breath. He paused for a few minutes on the porch, looking skyward and gave thanks. As an afterthought to his prayers, Ezra apologized to God because he had asked for someone to talk with. Ezra knew it was much too small a problem for God to consider.

Ezra stepped back inside, pushed the door closed with his foot and heard a voice. Or was his imagination running away with him? Then he heard it again.

A child's voice and it was coming from the loft, he was sure of it. "Hey, who's up there, show yourself," Ezra said, trying not to sound threatening.

A small round face with a tangle of red hair peeked over the edge of the loft and broke into a smile. "Hello, mister." And then another face looked through the log picket front of the loft.

It was the same face, only quite a few years older, a mother and child. "Sorry mister, but we were lost and cold, we come in during the night and kind of made ourselves at home, sorry, but we had nothing else."

Now it was Ezra's time to smile, "come on down, let's eat some breakfast and discuss how it was you ended up as guests in my guest loft."

The three talked and played games throughout the day. They made a cobbler from Ezra's dried berries and roasted a sage hen stuffed with wild onions. It wasn't much, by city standards, but the three feasted like royalty on that Christmas day.

It was late when Ezra pronounced himself talked out and ready for bed. All three turned in after one of the best Christmas's ever.

When Ezra walked out to the wood pile the next morning he didn't need to check, he knew they were gone. Breathing the rich mountain air he smiled, raised his hands to the heavens and said two words, "Thanks God." Then added, "Too talked out to say anything else."

Nobody ever saw or heard from Ol' Ezra again. No one is sure when or if he passed on. The cabin fell into ruin over the years.

If you hike that area, high up in the Wind River Mountains, and get to the ruins of the old cabin, stay for a while. Listen, listen very carefully and if the air is fresh and clear you might just hear it. Far off in the distance, or maybe right beside you, very faintly, three voices laughing and talking. Talking till they seemed all talked out.

~2~
Seven Red Bows at Christmas

Hardy Galloway pulled up rein, placed one knurled hand over the other on top his saddle horn and pushed back in an attempt to straighten his back. He was sore, sore and tired. He had not been on a horse in ten years, not until today. Not since Lucy died, hard to believe it had been ten years. Lucy was the best saddle horse he ever owned, didn't seem right to break in another after she passed.

Today was Hardy's sixtieth birthday. When he quit riding ten years ago, he believed 50 years old was too old to be in the saddle. The ranch lasted another three years; Hardy used the buggy or buckboard to go to town, which wasn't often. It was hard letting his hired men go. They were good ones, all four of them. To this day, he felt sorry that he let them go. But it was all he could do after selling off the cattle. Seven years ago and he thought he was old then, now 60, now what?

Two days before Christmas he decided he needed to go for a ride, a sixtieth birthday ride. Two hours ago Hardy saddled one of the three horses he kept around, and the only one broke to ride, a nice roan gelding. He swung up quickly; it felt good to be saddled and riding again. Now several miles from home, but still on his spread he wasn't so sure this was a good idea. But then again if he were home sitting in his rocking chair reading a book, as he spent most days, he would still be hurting, same as now.

He enjoyed reading, reading and rocking by the fireplace in the winter, and on the front porch in the summer. Reading the classics, with a few dime novels thrown in, helped pass the time of day and without knowing it, his life had passed also. Today everything had changed. After 16 growing up years, 37 ranch hand and ranch owner years, and finally seven years of rocking and reading his life was complete. Hardy never had children, never married, the ranch was his life and family, now his books were all he had. In a reflection of advancing years, he wasn't sure if it was enough. He'd helped people when they needed it and he never knowingly hurt anyone.

Hardy tapped his heels lightly, rode down a gentle slope, crossed an ancient buffalo wallow and stopped at a small stream. He gazed at azure blue water bubbling through coffee cup-sized ice flows. Like the classic authors who could find the perfect word, today he marveled at how nature could paint the perfect picture. A hawk cried out as it left its nearby roost breaking the moment.

He hated walking, hated it most all his adult life, but he dismounted took the reins in his hands and started walking along the stream. Somehow like riding today, walking felt good, felt right. How far he walked didn't matter but after what seemed to be an hour he felt more refreshed than tired. Hardy remounted and kicked the gelding into a trot and felt a smile on his weather-beaten face. Maybe he should do something for Christmas, after all it was only two days away.

Must be the Christmas stories he had been reading. Funny, but he enjoyed them even after not once in his life, doing anything for Christmas. Hardy was a good God fearing man and always enjoyed listening to the parson read the story of the birth of Christ at Christmas time. The Christmas stories he'd read the past few weeks were different, somehow as uplifting as the Bible story, maybe because he believed he was close to the end of his time on earth.

Hardy especially enjoyed Mark Twain's, *A Letter from Santa Claus*, which Twain wrote to his Daughter Suzy, who like her mother was sickly and had been since birth. Some of Hardy's friends read the work of Mark Twain, but none was aware of this short story. None of that mattered, the story was one of Hardy's favorites.

Turning back home the breeze stiffened, and Hardy pulled his coat up high under his chin. Doc had told him not to ride, said it could kill him, told him not to go out in the cold, might kill him. Hardy smiled at the irony; he was dying anyway, that's what the Doc said, might as well take a chance. He kicked the gelding into a trot, hollered a resounding hallelujah to the heavens and headed home.

It was a fine ride home, better than the ride out. Sure he hurt, but now he didn't care, he decided to live life instead of sit in that rocker reading about life. His plan? He did not have one, not yet, maybe sitting in the rocker and thinking would help.

Hardy jerked the reins startling the gelding and almost dismounting himself. It took a full minute to settle the horse then Hardy swung down from the saddle, patted his horse's neck and dropped the reins on the ground. He reached for the red ribbon in the sage and rubbed the material between his fingers. A red satin bow in the sage, puzzling did not begin to describe his thoughts at the moment.

He knew this country well, almost too well after all these years. His ride today was across his ranch, all except this small piece where he stood now holding a red satin bow. He'd ridden through this corner many times, the widow Melvin owned it, Kate Melvin. The last time he saw Kate was the year he sold his herd, seven years ago.

Her small ranch cornered into his; he owned the land on two sides and part of it on a third. Funny at one time they were friendly often spending time talking out on the range. They would see each other in church and sometimes at the monthly Saturday night socials. They danced so much together a few years ago that rumors circulated that they were a couple. It embarrassed Hardy, embarrassed him so bad he never went back to a Saturday night dance again.

Been a lot of years since he had been around Kate. He'd pushed her out of his mind, or tried to push her out because he cared for her, people noticed, and he was embarrassed. Seven years now since he danced with her, seven years since he spoke to her. Two months after their last dance he sold his cattle and retired. Retired to a life alone.

Nostalgia, Hardy wasn't sure if it was good to remember or not. Those had been tough times, not the cattle but losing Kate and never going back. Too late now, he thought. For a moment, he pondered taking the bow, but he couldn't, it didn't just tumble here in the wind. Hardy had a tough time getting in the saddle; everything hurt.

Now he rode slowly, unsure what hurt the most, his body or his spirit. Less than forty yards later, another bow and in a bit another. Seven in all, spaced, but not too far apart and all in the corner. Hardy had no idea where they came from or why they were there. Then he remembered it was only two days until Christmas. Someone, likely Kate, wanted to do a little decorating, but for whom?

Hardy turned to his right and rode up a small wooded rise, the only spot in the corner where he could see Kate Melvin's place. He had forgotten how breathtaking the setting for her cabin was. The rambling log home sat in a small open area surrounded by mature pine and cedar with a picture book stream winding past. Even from his vantage point of what he judged to be 150 yards he could see the bows. They were tied to the trees on either side of the front porch. At this distance, they were more of a red blur than a bow but instinctively, Hardy knew it, there were bows, dozens of them.

Now as the day took on the muted colors of a fading afternoon the bows seemed to be backlit, illuminated against the dark green of the trees. Hardy wanted to ride down, say hi, but he couldn't, not yet. A half hour later he grained his horse, turned her out in the corral and walked toward his house.

Too cool and with night about to pull the shade on another day Hardy stirred the fireplace coals and built a cozy fire. He walked outside and drug his rocking chair inside by the fire. He selected Anton Chekhov's, *"At Christmas Time."* It was in a book of Chekhov short stories, but oddly, although he knew it was there he had never read this one.

As he read on into the night, Hardy discovered not one, but two stories intertwined in an incredible Christmas tale. The first part was of a poor working class woman who hired a man to write a letter for her. She wanted to write a letter to her daughter and wish her a Merry Christmas. Her daughter had married and moved away four years earlier, and in the four years she had heard nothing.

Hardy read on and on; he had wished to read to relax, but this story was waking him instead of making him sleepy.

The second part of the story the daughter gets the letter, but her life is not what she or her parents expected. The story was most unsettling, and more about hopelessness, fear, and loneliness than anything else. Hardy's formally happy mood slipped away but more into reflection than sadness. He completely understood why this was a Christmas story with nothing of Christ or Santa Claus. It was about what matters, really matters in life. And maybe about being happy with who and where we are and happy with our station in life. The tale was one of relationships.

Hardy expected a sleepless night after all the goings on today. Instead he slept soundly, the best he could remember, at least the best he remembered since selling the ranch. He woke refreshed, dressed quickly and boiled coffee, poured a cup and walked outside. The air was cold; it was Christmas Eve morning, and he needed to write a letter.

My Dearest Kate, he started.

The letter took only minutes, not the hours that he expected. He folded it, placed it in a handmade envelope and sealed it with wax. As a final touch, Hardy took a small paint brush from a long forgotten hobby and put seven tiny red bows on the letter. He saddled the roan gelding and rode toward the Widow Melvin's.

He'd written the letter because he never felt good about his ability to speak of his feelings. He wanted her to read the letter, send him away or ask him to stay. He was not sure how much time he had, but what there would be of it, he wished to spend with a lady he had loved for twenty years and avoided for seven. He knew she would take her time reading it and might send him away while she thought about his proposal.

Hardy wanted to ride fast, and he wanted to ride slow, his emotions were mixed. He'd spent seven years of embarrassment and yesterday he knew for the first time he was embarrassed because he loved her. Her husband died in an accident cutting trees when he was in his twenties. Kate was a few years younger than him, but not many. She had been alone much of her adult life. Hardy was talking to himself as he rode speculating why a well to do, nice looking, and personable woman like Kate was still alone. Alone for so many years.

He hitched his horse to the rail near Kate's front porch, stepped up and knocked on the door. Chekhov's story of hope or hopelessness ran through his mind as Kate opened the door. It was that story pushing Hardy, last night, to a new understanding of his life

He had hope, his hope was Kate, but he needed to do something about it. "Hello Hardy, I've been expecting you, come on in," Kate said.

Hardy was dumbfounded, thinking, "Did she really say she was expecting me."

He was unsure how to start or what to say. Instead, he fumbled in his coat pocket for the letter. Kate waved him to a chair, leaned over and kissed him full on the mouth, smiled, walked into the kitchen and pulled two cups from a rack over the sink. Hardy sat with letter in hand, speechless.

The hot cocoa was delicious and unexpected; it had been years since the last time he'd tried it. Maybe it was the wonderful cocoa giving him courage, like an old-time gunfighter with a shot glass of whiskey in hand. He looked at Kate and smiled, then said the only thing he could think of. "You said you were expecting me, how could you have been expecting me, I'm glad you were, but"

Kate laughed, that infectious laugh, the one he'd thought of every day for seven years. She kneeled in front of him, crossed her arms on his knees and said, "When you disappeared from my life seven years ago, I was hurt and didn't understand, but I knew you would be back. Sometimes people need time, time to sort things out, I had so much hope you would come around. I was so sure that I would see you at Christmas seven years ago that I made a red bow and put it on the tree out front, but you never came. The second year I made another and I started putting them up on the hill thinking someday you might see one and wonder enough to come by."

Hardy began to say something but was shushed by Kate, who lightly touched the tip of her finger on his lips before continuing. "There are seven now seven red satin bows. On the fifth year I went through a sad time and tried to sew my way out of it, I worked an entire month making dozens of them, making them and trying to forget, forget what I thought we had."

Hardy reached out and put his hand on Kate's shoulder while he dabbed at his face with his neckerchief with the other. He was glad she continued because he was not at all sure he could talk at the moment.

"For a few days, just before Christmas each year, I put out the bows and ready the house for you and for Christmas. But don't be sad, right now seven years seems but a few days and now I am going to say what I should have seven years ago, Hardy Galloway, I love you, and I have loved you for thirty years."

Then a huge smile crossed her face, she stood and kissed him again and holding his hands she laughed. "Hardy I would have run off with you years ago, long before that scoundrel of a husband of mine passed on if you just would of asked."

Now it was Hardy's turn to talk, he stammered around before at last saying. "Well Kate, I guess I always loved you too, just never been much around women, guess it took me long enough."

They may have been too old, but to them age no longer mattered. Hardy told Kate of his health issues, but she explained that it did not matter because any time they had left was now time for both of them.

And you know what?

Hardy and Kate lived to see Wyoming become a state in 1890, and ten years later they took a break at midnight and held hands in the dance hall as the year 1900 was ushered in with their joy.

How long did they live?

They might still be there today, sitting on the porch of Kate's cabin in matched rocking chairs sipping hot cocoa.

A red bow covered pine danced in the breeze and all was good in the world, it was Christmas time.

~3~
A Most Magical Christmas

Light snow and slick in spots, that's what the weatherman on TV gave as the road report. Don't believe he stepped outside when he made that weather pronouncement about an hour ago.

Looks to me like there are already four or five inches of snow on the road and the longer I drive, the harder it seems to be coming down.

I thought it would be easy, only 60 miles and slick in spots should not take more than an hour and a half, even on bad roads. Now 30 minutes from home it was going to take longer might take a couple of hours, maybe more.

Twenty minutes later and another 10 or 12 miles, and I noticed the traffic was almost nonexistent. Guess they had a better weatherman that I did, or they had more sense.

The longer the highway seemed, the more I understood that driving today was a mistake. I hoped it would not become a huge mistake. Three weeks ago when I told my sister, "sure I'll be there," I was already muttering to myself, "Somehow I gotta get out of this," as I clicked off my phone.

Generally I don't mind kid's birthday parties, and I love spending time with my sister's family. It was only a few days before Christmas and like everyone else, I had many things left to do. But when she asked, "will you bring some of your magic stuff and do a few tricks for the kids?" Then in the same breath added, "Oh, and dress up in that funny, kind of clown outfit, that would be great, see you then."

That is how I reached my present station in life. Dressed in my, kind of a clown outfit, driving in what now was an absolute whiteout blizzard to do a few magic tricks and eat birthday cake with ice cream surrounded by giggling seven and eight-year-old girls.

Another hour and a half passed and I knew I was in trouble. I wanted to say, and instinctively I knew I was in trouble, like they do in the movies, but it didn't take any instincts to see that it was trouble for anyone out in this storm, no instincts needed.

Wyoming high country roads are, at best, unpredictable in winter, today they were just plain bad. The rest of this trip could take a few more minutes or several hours, the way my luck was turning, possibly years. What I could see through my windows was white, nothing else.

My car gave me the sensation of sliding, I hoped it was not real. Before I could make out anything in the snow to reference where the highway was, I heard the sickening thud of the car bottomed out in the roadside ditch. Cramping the wheel back left and stomped on the accelerator as hard as I could, the engine roared, the car lowered itself and stopped moving. There was no chance to drive out, but just in case, I pushed the accelerator to the floor for a second try. Yep, stuck.

There was no need to open the door, even if I could, the Mustang was buried. The snow was deep, two inches up on the side windows. Now what should I do?

After living all my life in Wyoming, I was no fool. I pulled my winter survival kit from the back seat: flashlight, three candy bars, two bottles of water, a silver metal looking blanket, clown shoes - wondered where I had put them, a pair of thick gloves and another coat, a heavy one. Do I stay or do I go, that is the question? Stuck and in a terrible situation and I still cannot stop from making bad clown jokes.

Deciding to wait and do nothing was an easy choice, do nothing, not yet anyway. I slid the seat all the way back and tried to stretch. I punched my sister's number into my cell and she picked up immediately. "You're not attempting to drive in this blizzard are you?" "Ahh, kind of," I said.

The phone was silent long enough that I thought maybe she'd hung up, then, "you're stuck aren't you?"

"Yep!"

Silence from my sister again, followed by a pained, "where are you?"

I looked around, everything looked the same, white. "In the right-hand ditch, maybe eight or ten miles out."

She sighed, I hate it when she sighs, she's been doing that to me since we were kids, and it always meant the same thing. "What were you thinking?"

She said, "Stay where you are, I'll see if I can find a snowplow going that way so we can send a wrecker out, this is supposed to blow through in the next hour or so." I said, "Okay," and hung up.

I started to shiver and twisted the key and listened as the engine and the heater came to life, then wondered if the same weather man that said roads would be slick in spots was the one now saying, "It will blow through in the next hour or so?"

Five minutes later I reclined my seat as far as it would go, shut off the engine and tried to relax for a short wait. I knew my, stuck and waiting time, could become longer depending on road conditions and how many others were in my same predicament. I dug out my duffel bag, the one with the magic tricks in it, deciding to do a little practice while I waited. A few minutes later, bored of entertaining myself, I stuck the magic tricks along with the clown shoes in the duffel and tossed it on the back seat.

The early evening changed from dark as a cave at midnight, to a full moon and stars lighting up the snow. Now it seemed almost daylight and the snow had stopped. No wind and eerily quiet as I tried digging my way out of the car. I know, I said I would stay put, but now it's pretty nice out, time to go. Why not walk down the road a ways, maybe walk all the way to town, and surprise my sister?

It took ten minutes to dig enough snow away from the car to get the door open. Thought about crawling out of the window, like they do in the movies, but I have kind of, shall we say, got away from exercise lately. Might have been more than a little embarrassing to have someone find me stuck in the window of my Mustang.

The snow was knee deep, not as bad as I thought. I had on my boots, the ones I always wore when I went out in the winter, you didn't believe I was going to pull on my clown shoes for a snow walk did you? I pulled my stocking hat down tight and flipped my hood up and over and I was off. Not bad, not bad at all. The snow was somewhat above my knees now, but I was pretty sure I was walking on the road, and almost certain I was heading the correct way toward my sisters and not away from it.

An hour, perhaps an hour and a half had passed before I knew, really knew, I was in trouble, my feet were numb and crusted with snow and I was starting to shiver. I'd checked on other cars as I walked, four or five, I no longer could remember. Seems to be getting colder, much colder and the wind is starting to blow. Too late and too far to go back.

Another abandoned car was stuck in the left-hand ditch if only I could get inside and warm up – locked. I slumped down in the snow but out of the wind by the car's front fender and decided to take a nap. Renew my energy.

Not sure when I recognized the fact it was no longer cold. But I felt warm and comfortable. Without thinking, I reached out and picked up a cup of hot chocolate and took a warm, soothing sip. Looking around, this might seem crazy, but I was in some kind of workshop. A workshop like all those storybook pictures of Santa's workshop I'd seen as a kid.

I was still clear-headed enough to know that I must be dreaming, but then again, there he was, Santa, sitting not 20 feet away. He was smiling, surrounded by elves as he put together a tiny wooden train. This was real, or at least seemed to be, how did I get here? I was working in a toy workshop, Santa's workshop. Working with a bunch of elves, I never believed could be real.

It's a dream, help, this story is turning into one of those, it's only a dream stories. I really don't like any of the, it was only a dream stories. How did I get here? But this one is not a dream, all of this is too real, much too real.

I remember walking from my car, getting colder and colder and sitting down. I froze to death. I'm dead. I must be in heaven. I didn't know that heaven was at the North Pole. Something isn't right here, not right at all.

Someone tapped my shoulder. "Are you on strike today or what?"

I turned and a very grumpy Elf was giving me a most stern look. "What, what was that you said," I mumbled?

"I said are you working or just sitting and drinking hot chocolate today, we have deadlines you know!"

I nodded, and for the first time looked at the table in front of me, address labels, wrapping paper and books, stacks and stacks of books laid out in front of me. Wasn't sure, but evidently my job, and I am not sure how I got a job here, was to write names on labels and wrap the books.

A fat tablet in front of me had names, list after list of names. Picking up a giant red marker I carefully wrote the first name, Mae, on the label and looked at the books, selecting, "*Zombies Live in My Back Yard*," and wrapped it in bright mirror-like red paper. Looking over my shoulder, the Elf must have been satisfied, he was gone. Guess wrapping and writing labels is my job. I went back to work.

Grabbing a green marker, I printed, Mady, wrapped a book titled, "*Girls in Space*, "and placed it on my, now two-book high finished pile. Blue marker, "Bryley," I was getting good at this job. Let's see, "*Adventures in Vampire Hunting*, "wrapped and placed on the pile, I looked up, no one was watching me any longer.

Hours later my stack of books to wrap was still taller than my ready to go pile. Every time the finished pile started to look pretty good an ancient looking woman brought a pile of new books along with a new supply of labels, sat them on the table and took away the wrapped ones. This job was much harder than I thought it was going to be.

"Mister, mister, you all right in there? Mister?"

Highway Patrol, it said on the man's uniform patch. I wasn't dead, I wasn't in heaven, I wasn't frozen to death, and I didn't need to wrap any more presents in Santa's workshop. I was alive and ready to go to my niece's birthday party and do a few magic tricks.

Minutes later a wrecker pulled the Mustang and me from the clutches of the snow. The patrolman reminded me the road was slick and commended me for, "staying put and not getting out of the car and trying to walk out of here, like some of the crazies do."

"No not me officer," I said, "I'm not one of the crazies, no way I would try and walk out of here."

I drove along the cleared but still snow packed and dangerous road at 35 miles-per-hour. I reached for my coffee cup knowing it would be cold, but I needed the caffeine jolt. Funny the cup felt warm in my hand when I picked it up, this is one great cup, I thought.

I took a drink, it was wonderful and it was hot and it was not coffee, it was hot chocolate. I smiled, thinking I must have got hot chocolate instead of coffee at the quick stop. That must be the reason I had that weird dream of the North Pole and Santa's workshop. Yep, the dream I was having when I was not being one of those crazies trying to walk away from a car stuck in two feet of snow.

Ten minutes later I was parked in front of the birthday girl's house.

Party time.

My sister gave me a big hug and a kind of, you might be crazy look, but seemed happy to see me. My niece was her usual bubbly self, running to greet me and telling me as if I didn't know, that today was her birthday and it really snowed hard a little while ago. With that welcome, she went back into the family room with her friends.

Opening the bag of tricks, duffel bag I took out the present I had so carefully shopped for, bought and wrapped. Odd, I didn't remember bringing other presents, but there they were, in my bag of tricks. Three expertly wrapped gifts, looked and felt like books of some kind. Funny, but they looked a lot like the books from my dreams.

Hum – three extra presents and three friends here for the birthday party. Maybe I could give all the kids a present, not just my niece. Carefully I pulled the name tags from the presents, Mady, Bryley and Mae, I shook my head the names sounded familiar. Oh – well, I was ready to be the greatest uncle ever.

Looking up four young ladies were walking toward me. "So," I said, looking at my niece, "who are your little friends?"

She looked at me with her best, close to serious look, and said. "You've met them before," and then with as much grandeur as she could assume, "this is Bryley, this is Mady and this is Mae.

Hearing those names, I don't believe I passed out, but I should have. I reached into my bag of tricks, quickly re-stuck the name tags and took out the presents. "Of course I remembered your friends, tricked you, didn't really think I would ever forget your best friends did you?"

I handed all four of the girls their presents and watched, with delight, as they opened them. Those book titles sure did sound familiar, must have been something from the dream.

That night was now seemed a lifetime ago, 10 years. I'm still not sure what happened on that snow packed Wyoming highway and not sure I want to know. But it was a great birthday party and all my tricks worked to perfection for the one and only time.

Yes, it was a most magical evening, most magical indeed

~4~
The Workshop Was Bare

The workshop was nearly bare. Nick had laid off most of his workers months ago and last week the rest were let go. Oh sure, Nick told them it would be a temporary layoff, but he felt like that was a lie. He told them anyway, it made him feel better, and he really did hope for the best. These were tough times, and Nick realized he may have to lay himself off, close the shop, perhaps bankruptcy. Just thinking about it turned his stomach.

First his grandfather and then his father had thrived in this business and Nick had doubled the workforce and doubled the income in the first decade he'd ran the business, and now this. He blamed it on the economy and he blamed it on people who no longer believed in the magic of Christmas. They didn't buy as much as they once had and when they bought for Christmas, it was video games and electronics, not the old-fashioned wooden toys he was so proud of making in his, one of a kind, shop.

"What's wrong with good solid handmade toys," he said more often than he needed. "They'll last a lifetime, maybe two lifetimes." But no one listened, not anymore.

He didn't want, or need, an answer, he knew the answer. Society, like everything else, changes. As the years pass, so do fads and fancies. His toys were no longer part of American dreams, children passed them by for flashier and more sophisticated things. But what did he know about trends and society, he still smoked an old brier-wood pipe, and when Martha wasn't watching, dumped a packet of peanuts in his Pepsi. He still wore real leather boots and belts, preferred wool winter socks to the new space-age materials. And he loved to laugh and to talk and to sing, seemed to Nick like there was not enough laughter, talking or singing anymore.

47 years old was not too old to start over, but Nick was not sure how, or what if he were to begin again. For now Nick sat at his work table attaching tiny wooden wheels to the last of the four dozen trains he had made, mostly by himself, this year.

So many wooden toys over the years, so much joy for so many kids. Nick was not sure he could, or would want to do anything but make wooden, trains, planes, cars, and buildings. His mind wandered as he worked on the train and he thought of Christmas seasons past.

Must have dozed off, Nick thought, he rubbed his eyes and looked around his empty workshop. But it wasn't empty, not by any stretch of the imagination, it was full. Full of workers and full of toys. People and toys were everywhere, stacked in every corner, toys not the workers.

Nick thought he remembered having a Pepsi sitting on the table next to him, he needed a drink. He reached for the soda and found a steaming cup of hot chocolate instead with dozens of tiny marshmallows not yet melted. His hand trembled a bit as he picked it up and took a small sip, it was delicious, the best he had ever tasted. He couldn't remember the last time he'd drank hot chocolate, must have been when he was a kid. No wonder it tasted so good, it had been too long. He looked around to see if anyone was watching him, looking for a reaction, but everyone was working, smiling, talking and happy.

Nick felt an itch on his chin and reached to scratch, he had a beard. This was odd, most odd, he had always been clean shaven, never had a beard. Nick walked over toward the water cooler, the one with the big mirror above it, he had to see what he looked like in a beard.

It was a good thing the water cooler was sturdy, actually it was a drinking fountain, looked like the same one he remembered replacing years ago. Nick held onto the ancient fountain and looked around, then he looked back into the mirror. This cannot be happening, has to be a dream!

The beard was thick, must have taken a year to grow, at least a year. And it was long, most long and white, very white. He looked like Santa Clause, this better be a dream. Nick didn't want to wake up, this was fun, except for the goofy red suspenders he saw in the mirror, he couldn't remember owning a pair, they had to go.

He steadied himself, then walked back to his desk and started painting the roof leading up to a steeple on a tiny white church. He couldn't remember when he had started painting the tiny church, but he must have. The paint, paint brush and the small wooden church were all there, on his desk, right in front of him.

As he used the brush to paint marks to look like shingles, he could feel before he could see someone standing beside him. He put his paintbrush down and turned toward them. No one was there. Oh, yes there was, but they were not very tall. It was an elf, a little lady elf.

This dream was turning from fun to weird, strange indeed. But Nick wasn't ready to wake up, not yet. He turned to the elf and said, "What can I do for you Trally-Mae?"

Nick felt an electric shock, not a real one, or at least he didn't think it was real. How did he know her name? Nick had never heard of anyone named Trally-Mae.

"Mr. Nick, we are out of, coconut, chocolate chips, and cinnamon and have not yet finished making candy. Is it okay if we take the sleigh and make a run to the South Pacific and pick some up?"

Nick looked dumbfounded, and she quickly added, "Just kidding."

Nick was temporarily speechless, didn't know what to say if he could have talked, so he only mumbled, "could you get me some more hot chocolate, please?" Trally-Mae nodded and vanished.

Nick closed his eyes, not looking for sleep, but to wake up. This had to be a dream, much too crazy to be real. He pinched his eyes shut as tight as he could get them and told himself he would not open them until his old world came back.

Then a thought came, his old world was bad, dreadfully bad. He had to lay off all his workers, kids didn't like his toys anymore and he was sad in his big empty shop. Nick popped open his eyes, nothing had changed. Workers and elves were everywhere, working, singing, whistling, happy workers.

Nick didn't want this to end, he started to whistle, stopped for a drink of hot chocolate and then began to hum. He looked around, the workers he had laid off were all there, among the elves and some workers he had never seen. They were all making wooden toys, oh- except for the elves, they were making candy. He had never been so happy.

Nick closed his eyes one more time, opened them to the same scene and setting he had closed them to. This was his life and a good life it was.

Nick Claus smiled, took his old briar wood pipe from his pocket, laid it on his work table and sipped his hot chocolate. Looked around for Martha, didn't see her, and poured a sack of peanuts into a shiny new can of Pepsi. If this was a dream, he might as well have his all-time favorite snack.

The dream must have been about him being a third generation wooden toy maker in the process of going broke, sure was some nightmare. He picked up his paint brush and reminded himself to cut back on the extra cookies, they might be the cause of his bad dreams.

He dunked a sugar cookie in his hot chocolate, took a bite, and smiled. He sipped from the Pepsi and peanuts then placed it carefully beside the hot chocolate. He put his elbows on the table and folded his hands under his chin, looked out over his workshop – life was great, especially if you are Santa Clause.

~5~
A Wyoming Christmas Tale

Luke Charles didn't feel much like Thanksgiving. Thanksgiving and Christmas had once been a time of, at least, some joy in his life. Now he did not care, he could never be happy again, or at least he felt that way. The cold air made it feel more like December than it did a few days ago. After weeks of very mild days, winter was at last pushing a lingering fall out of the air. Luke didn't know what day or what month it was, Thanksgiving time maybe, or early December, he thought, sometime in the first week or maybe the second, he wasn't sure. That would make Christmas only two or three weeks away. He didn't feel like rejoicing, he felt much the opposite, didn't really matter if it was Thanksgiving or Christmas. He rode on in silence and disappointment.

He had worked hard building his LC spread and then things turned sour. It all started over a year ago when he bought those damned Texas cows. Along with the cows came the tick fever and he lost his herd. All that was left were two yearling bulls and three heifers. Those five might make a pretty good start for some, but he had already done that, nine years before. Nine years to build his herd and one season to destroy it, and then two more months to destroy his life.

Now he was riding away, to where he did not know and did not care. He thought that he might be in western Nebraska with the rolling hills and small streams every few miles, but he wasn't sure. Maybe he had stayed on that Wyoming ranch for too long after the cattle died, should have left right away and went back home to Pennsylvania. But he loved that mountain valley ranch on the Big Horn River. It had all seemed so perfect when he and Lila had moved west more than a decade ago. Could it have been that long? And could it have been that perfect?

Luke stopped by another of the nameless streams and unsaddled his spotted Indian pony. That pony, the clothes he was wearing, his rifle and .45 were about all that was left of his life on the ranch. His life had been mostly fulfilling and wonderful just a few months ago.

The small thicket of plum brush and scrub Cottonwood looked to be as good a place as any and he tied the pony near the stream where it could graze, on what little grass was left, and drink. Luke started to gather some of the smaller Cottonwood falls to build a fire. The grass had turned brown with just a few of the less desirable stems holding onto some fall green. But it was a beautiful day and the pony seemed to enjoy eating the tough, sparse, leftover greens. Luke cupped his hands and sipped water from the stream, finding it sweet and cold he filled his canteen. He fetched the coffee pot and dug the small skillet from his saddle bags.

Tossing the little bit of bacon he had left into the skillet, he smiled a rare smile when it popped and sizzled. The aroma was overwhelming, hunger pangs were biting; it had been since last night when he had stopped long enough to eat.

He had no idea why he was moving so fast. He was not a wanted man and there shouldn't be anyone looking for him, not for any reason he could think off anyway. But he remained cautious, looking around as he cooked and thought. Luke sat on the trunk of an ancient downed tree with a trunk worn smooth as the flat rocks in the little stream. What the stream water never had a chance to do, years of exposure to sun and wind had. It was one of a half-dozen downed trees in the area; Luke imagined a tornado or lightning flattening the trees long before he was born. He looked around again and for a brief moment thought, why?

Why did the trees come down and why am I so worried? If someone is after me they could just kill me and get it over with, somehow in his mind it seemed to be a possibility that he could accept, just more bad luck to run out the streak, he thought. Just like these poor trees, standing one day, down the next and now good only to cook his meager evening meal. He poked at the fire and continued thinking about the past, hurtful, and the future, hopeless.

Luke stood, turned a small circle then stretched, pulled his Colt, checked the cylinders, tried to twirl it and then slid it back into the holster. He reached with both hands behind his back, stretching, trying to ease the lower back pain brought on from too many nights under the stars and too many hours on horseback. He was tense, but his mind stayed alert, just in case. Luke pulled his rifle from the saddle scabbard, levered in a shell and pointed it toward a distant tree. He drew his .45 again and pointed it toward his imaginary target, put his thumb on the hammer of the single-action sidearm then lowered it and dropped it straight into his holster. Nerves, he thought, not sure why?

He squatted by the fire again and tore strips of jerky into smaller pieces making sure they were the nice bite size pieces he liked. As he tore the stringy meat, he tossed each small chunk into the skillet. Taking his canteen, he poured water into the mixture of bacon and jerky and then sprinkled in some flour, all the time stirring his dinner. It wasn't much, but it was what he had, and that would do, same as it had for the past months.

Four months, it had been four months since he had ridden south from that Big Horn valley ranch, traveled south and never looked back. Not even a look back to see if the fire he started, just outside the bedroom, had taken. Luke hoped so, didn't want anyone to inherent his troubles or his memories, from the LC Ranch. Four months since the fever had taken Lila, the worst four months of his life.

He had ridden south, blaming himself for the loss of his wife nearly every step of the way, for two weeks before turning east, then back south and now he was going northeast. No particular reason just wandering. Unlike most wanderers he steered clear of towns, ranches and homesteaders, only going into town when he needed supplies. He sipped the near boiling coffee and leaned back against the stump of an ancient cottonwood and thought. Luke liked to remember the better times but seldom could. The memories of the ranch and his wife and the dreams were not as vivid as they had been, but they were still there. Luke was not sure if he wanted them to go away or to stay.

The dreams were the worst, so real that Luke woke up hoping that the bad things were the dream and the dream was real. But after every dream he woke up alone on his bedroll and disappointed. He seemed to think more about the ranch and the cows than he did of Lila and maybe that was part of the bad memories. She never really took to the ranch or ranch life and instead of growing closer they had seemed to grow more distant each year. More distant until the end when she got sick, then they became as close as when they were newlyweds, but there was not enough time. She was gone so quickly, almost as soon as the cows.

Luke cleaned his plate with sand and dead grass then rinsed it in the stream. The meal had fixed his hunger, but he looked around and was not satisfied. Not with his life, not with any part of it. He was still alone, all alone, and not sure if he wanted it any other way.

After yet another night full of happy dreams of the past and waking up alone, cold and hungry, knowing that his past could never be again. Luke took another look at the sky and thought it was starting to lighten. Dawn could not be that far away. He packed his belongings, saddled the paint and rode off. Back toward the ranch, he wasn't sure why.

Four months was not enough grieving time for Luke Charles, he felt like a full lifetime would not be enough to grieve for everything he had lost, but he was heading for the ranch in the Big Horn Basin. The ranch where he had spent most of the good years of his life. He was not going back to live or even to stay for a spell. He was going back because he had too. Not to see if the house had burned, he had long since given up the notion of calling it a home and only thought of it as a house. No, this was more personal, maybe one last good-bye as he felt the memories start to slip from his mind and he fought to try to keep them. It was time.

It took another three and a half weeks to reach the ranch, a ride of almost three hundred miles. Luke took his time giving his horse much-needed rests and taking the time to let his mind relax from the worries of the past months. He had come to think of himself as a wanderer over the past half year, but the last few weeks he had begun to see a direction for the first time in months. Not a direction to ride the paint horse but maybe a direction to his life.

Luke wasn't sure what he thought when he rode up the ridge south of his old place; he stopped and tied the paint then walked the last fifty yards to where he could look over on so many memories. He looked down and saw his place, smoke coming from the chimney, the corral looked repaired and solid and he could see a small bunch of cows near the back of the barn. North of the old corrals were two new pens, each holding a few fine looking horses, and what appeared to be the start of a new shed?

Someone had moved in and he felt, well, he wasn't sure how he felt. Happy he guessed, maybe relieved. He would never live there again and he didn't want the place back, he just needed to bury, at last, some memories.

He walked back remounted and rode down into the yard, calling out as he rode, "Hey neighbor."

A woman stepped out onto the porch running her fingers over her forehead, brushing thick dark brown hair away from her face then using the hand as a shield against the glare of the afternoon sun. "Something I could do for you, mister?" Before she finished speaking, two boys that looked to be less than five or six year's old followed mom onto the porch.

Luke pulled off his hat and said faster than he intended. "Don't want to be a bother, but I used to live around here and was just passing through, or truth is I rode over here to see just how this old place looked, is the man of the house about?"

The young mother reached out, as if in slow motion, wrapping an arm around the shoulders of her two young boys and pulled them close, looking down as she answered. "No man, not anymore, he left heading to Casper most of three months ago and never came back. I knew something bad had happened, but I didn't want to admit it. Rider stopped by three weeks back, gave us the news."

Luke felt the, now familiar, lump in his stomach like he was going to be sick. "This place is cursed," he blurted out before he took the time to reconsider and remain quiet.

The woman on the porch took her hand away from her forehead and looked up at him, surprised at his outburst. "No, I don't think so, someone put in a lot of work here and then left it all, not cursed, just a lot of hard work. I feel like maybe I should know who you are, but I'm sure I've never laid eyes on you before." She closed her eyes, as if in deep thought or prayer, for just a few seconds and then said, "You built this place didn't you?"

Luke was caught off guard by the quick study she had made of him and wondered if his life was really that transparent. "Seems like a long time ago, I don't mean to come here and take the place back, you've proved up, tougher than I was. I guess I just needed one last look, not sure what I was expecting, though."

"Enough, that's enough of the past, why don't you unsaddle and take supper with us? I was about to make biscuits when we heard you ride up, no problem to make a few more, you like biscuits and roast beef don't you?" Then as an afterthought, she added, "I got an apple pie in the oven, for tomorrow. And after you accept my supper invitation, please, call me Mary."

Luke had already climbed down and reached for the cinch, then stopped looked up and asked. "Why tomorrow, one day to eat something as good as apple pie seems as good as any other doesn't it?"

Mary stopped in mid-door, turned and looked at Luke. He felt his face warming as he started to blush. He reached under his horse to undue the saddle cinch and to hide his face and heard her say as she closed the door.

"Tomorrow is Christmas."

Luke wasn't sure if he should feel good right now, his mind was racing, maybe he should feel bad, real bad, still. He tried to sort out his thoughts but knew how he did feel; better, better than any time since he left. He wasn't sure why. Luke led his paint horse around to the shed roofed barn he had built more than five years ago and put him in a familiar stall, noticing how well it had been kept since he left. Clean, neat and repaired. He hung his saddlebags from a nail above the stall and shook his head thinking that, at the moment that was all he owned, a horse and whatever he could fit on its back.

Luke took extra time to wash up from the pump near the barn before heading to the house for his first sit-down supper in almost six months. He wished he had a clean shirt, but he didn't, so he settled for a quick brush up and down with the palms of his hands and a re-tuck into his trousers. He walked a few steps then stopped, stood on one leg and alternated wiping the top of each boot on the back of opposite pant leg. Two times with each boot but they didn't look any better. He shook his head walked up to the house, tapped his knuckles twice and opened the door.

He could smell the apple pie from just outside the horse barn but in the house it overwhelmed everything, he could sit here and enjoy this for quite a long spell. Mary directed him to a chair at what he considered to be the head of the table. He declined but Mary insisted and he sat down, at the same place he had sat so many times when this was his home and his house.

The table was pushed up against the cabin wall so that there were chairs at the head and foot of the table and two smaller, but higher chairs set up against the open, long side of the table. The two children sitting there were boys. As he looked at the boys, Mary introduced them as Arthur and Aaron. "Arthur usually says grace as he is the man of the house now, but you being the guest, seems only proper that you give thanks, after you properly introduce yourself that is."

Luke felt his face flush for the second time in half an hour and quickly bowed his head hoping they would follow and not see his embarrassment. There was something about this lady that he really liked or didn't like, he wasn't sure which. Luke had not been much of a praying man until he lost the herd and then Lucy, after that he prayed a lot. First he prayed that the good Lord would bring everything back, then that he could die and be done with it, and at last, mad torturing prayers, where he screamed at the sky blaming God for all his troubles. Then after a few weeks he gave up on prayers and he gave up on God, opened his saddlebag and tossed his small *Bible* into the Wyoming sage and gave up, almost on everything.

"Lord we do truly thank you for this day and for this food which looks more than a might better than I'm used to, but then I'm not much of a cook and looks like Mary here is. Amen"

He opened his eyes and saw the others at the table looking at him and smiling. He felt the now familiar warmth in his face start for the third time today. "Oh, I'm Luke, Luke Charles, and you're right, I built this place, me and my wife, she's gone now."

"Why'd you leave?"

"Couldn't stay, not after I lost everything and I'm not staying now, the place is yours, you and the boys. But it's a fearful place as I guess you already know a fearful place, fearful."

Mary passed Luke a steaming china plate of biscuits followed by a gray platter with a large beef roast stacked to the edges. She handed him a pair of butcher knives and asked if he would cut meat for the boys. He served them first then cut a piece for himself, smaller than he really wanted and then self-consciously handed the platter to Mary so that she could help herself last. Somehow he didn't think she should be last, more fitting she should have taken hers first, Luke felt his face growing hot again. The past hour his face had turned to embarrassed red so often that he hoped she would think his was sunburned, not likely in December, but maybe. Then when he realized that he was more worried about what Mary thought about his red face than the red face itself he felt the color darkening even more. He put his head down and started shoveling the food, from plate to mouth, like he had not eaten a proper meal for quite some time - which he had not.

Luke thought the meal was incredible, maybe it was hunger or maybe it was the excellent company. The pie was delicious and a fitting finish to the meal, he declined a second piece out of politeness, but he wished he had not declined. Maybe he could get that second piece before he left this place in the morning. That is if she asked him to stay and if she invited him to breakfast. He really didn't relish the idea of sleeping in the open again; the bunkhouse sure would be nice.

Mary was picking up dishes before Luke realized maybe he should ask if she needed help. "Here let me help you do that."

She shook her head and continued to clean up, stopping as she reached for Luke's coffee cup. "I want you to do something for me, didn't seem right 'till today, will you cut us a Christmas tree?"

"Sure," Luke said.

Then he felt the now, all too familiar, warmth as his face flushed once again.

"I know it sounds frivolous, but the boys would like it, I would too, and use the bunkhouse, stay for Christmas tomorrow. No one, no matter how bad times are, should be alone at Christmas."

Luke just nodded opened the door and walked toward the woodshed to get an ax.

It took more time to pick a tree than to cut it down, Luke was familiar with the location of about every pine and juniper in miles and he knew where he could find just what he needed for Christmas. Somehow, someway he was excited about the prospect of Christmas morning and he wanted the perfect tree. He was back in less than two hours, dropped the tree on the front porch, put his horse away, and walked the few steps to the bunkhouse. Time to slow down and think, sort things out, if he could.

There were four hand-hewn beds in the bunkhouse, Luke started a fire in the stove and stretched out on the bunk closest to the fire. It didn't seem like he had laid there long, maybe only a few minutes or maybe he had dozed off, he wasn't sure when he heard a knock on the door. Startled he sat up, rubbed his eyes and called out, "come on in."

Mary was not sure about coming in, but she did open the door, peek in and say, "come on up to the house, Christmas Eve, we need to celebrate and set up the tree." She closed the door and walked away quickly, embarrassed, but with a smile on her face she was not sure would ever go away.

Luke walked to the barn to check on his horse and Mary's livestock wishing all the way that he had something he could give as a present to the boys. But he knew that he had nothing, nothing that even looked like a gift and no time to make or buy something. He patted his horse wishing he had something sweet for him, like a Christmas gift he thought, but he didn't even have that. Luke closed the door, secured it for the night and walked toward the house.

What is going on he thought, this seems so right but I know it is every bit of wrong. He knocked on the house door and it swung wide with two smiling boys fighting over who got to pull it open. The smell in the house he could not identify, but it smelled fantastic, it smelled like Christmas when he was growing up back home in Ohio.

Mary handed Luke a steaming cup of what he decided was apple cider with cloves, the smell had been great, and the taste was even better. She went back to the oven and took out another pie even though he could see a quarter of the pie from earlier still warming above the stove.

"Ever since I was a kid I liked special treats on Christmas and here is mine for this year, it's a rhubarb and raspberry pie, it's from my summer put ups, hope you like it."

Half an hour, three cups of cider and two pieces of pie later, Luke was stuffed and sleepy. He didn't know why, but he felt like he was drunk. Now he had been drunk before and wasn't proud of it, but this time it was something else. The house was warm his belly was full; he was happy and he felt great, maybe the best he'd felt since he was a kid. He looked at Mary and wondered if she felt like he did, not the full stomach part because he had not seen her eat a thing. But she did look happy. They sat smiling at each other, watching the boys as they ate, playing and tussling with each other.

Luke and Mary couldn't take their eyes from one another, telling stories of their lives to each other and to the boys. He was drunk all right, how else could any reasonable man fall in love in one afternoon after months of mourning. He knew he was in love, just not sure what to do next. Luke was not sure if he should leave or stay, he thought he should run away and mourn, but he wanted Mary to ask him to stay and for more than just one night.

Mary, Luke, and the boys spent a good two hours stringing popcorn and placing it on the tree. Mary also owned a few Christmas decorations that the four of them put on and around the tree. Much too soon Luke knew it was time for him to go to his temporary quarters for the night. He tried to say his goodnights but was interpreted by Mary, "but Luke you need to read the Christmas story to us, we need to hear it on Christmas Eve."

Mary opened the *Bible* to *Luke 2, Chapter 1* and handed it to the modern day Luke, could he be anything like the biblical Luke, she wondered? Luke, the beloved physician, mentioned in Colossians. He was not a doctor but maybe he was a healer, maybe he was the answer she had been praying for.

Luke read the familiar story, closed the *Bible*, said goodnight and headed to the barn to check on the stock, one last time, before going to bed. He laughed, knowing this was the second, one last time of the evening. The stars and the moon were bright and a fresh snowfall made the night almost as bright as day. Luke stopped and looked at one star that outshone all the others. The North Star maybe, he thought, or the star of Bethlehem, the one he had just read about. Was this trying to tell him something or was he making impossible connections because he wanted something impossible to happen?

Luke swung open the barn door, patted along the door frame and found the lamp, twisted the wick up and lit it, adjusted it slightly and walked toward the horse stalls. He tipped the light forward to see his paint horse better, rubbing his eyes as he tried to adapt to the dim yellow light cast from the lamp. Did he see shadows? He took several quick steps to see what looked like something resting on his paint horses back. He was sure he had taken the saddle and bed role from the horse hours ago, he was reassured when he could see that they were still there, hanging on the stall where he had left them. Luke reminded himself to take the bedroll and guns to the bunkhouse before he patted the cold nose of the paint stallion and looked at a large brown burlap bag, a bag full of what appeared to be various sized boxes tied to his horse's back.

Luke looked around to see if this was some kind of a joke being played on him but he knew that it was not. He took the sack from the horses back, laid it in clean straw outside the stall and carefully dumped out the contents. Packages wrapped in brown paper and tied with red and green ribbons, labeled, for him and Mary and one for each of the boys. He was sure that Mary put them here but not sure why. But when, she had not left the house? He had been with her since the last time he had checked the horses, several hours ago, and there were no packages then. And to further confuse the matter, neither of the children had left the house either, only him, and he did not tie a bundle of packages to the back of his own horse.

Luke carried the bag with the four packages back to the bunkhouse, sat down on his bed and thought about the day; he was not sure what was going on. Luke closed his eyes and held them shut tight for a few seconds opened them and looked at the packages; they were still there where he had put them, still on the floor in front of him. He was not dreaming. Luke shook his head hoping to clear something, he was not sure what, from his still whirling brain. He took the three steps from his bunk to the door and cracked it open looking out toward the now dark ranch house.

It was time, time to deliver the presents, the gifts from where, he did not know. There was a new cover of snow as Luke walked toward the house. His boots reminded him how cold it was as they squeaked with every footstep he placed in the new white crystals. It had been a long time since Luke had thought about the days as a kid when he and his brother laughed at the funny squeaking sound their shoes made in the snow when it was freezing cold. With temperatures near zero, he remembered, but wished he could be a little quieter.

But it didn't matter, Luke eased open the front door and could not hear a sound. He crept to the small Christmas tree and placed the presents underneath, noticing that there were other presents already there. He turned to leave and Mary stood blocking his way standing in the doorway. Luke was not sure how she got there or why she was there, but there she was. "Now just where would a footloose and fancy-free man like yourself come up with a sack full of Christmas presents on Christmas Eve, thought you just happened upon the old place again?"

Luke flushed again, thinking she was mad as he tried to stutter out some kind of explanation, then he noticed the twinkle in her eyes and the smile creeping across her mouth. "How'd you do it, how did you get those presents out to the barn and strapped across my horse?"

Now it was Mary's turn to be puzzled, "now see here Mr. Charles, if this is some kind of a joke," she never finished the thought. Luke reached for her hand, when she took it, he pulled her close.

They walked, holding hands out the door to the porch. Neither seemed to mind the cold as they stood and looked at the sky, now clear, and twinkling with hundreds of bright Christmas Eve stars. "I need to walk down to the barn, got to see who brought those presents, if neither of us did, someone did," Luke said.

Mary opened the door and grabbed her wrap and the two walked arm in arm toward the barn, neither saying a word.

Somewhere about half-way between the house and the barn the two stopped and held each other. They held tight with bitter cold snow crystals falling, letting the bad pass from their lives and all that seemed right to enter. After what seemed to be several minutes Mary pushed away slightly, tipped her head back and pulled Luke to her, kissing him softly. Luke returned the kiss with a passion he was not sure he had ever had before, or if he had, it was long since forgotten.

Now they walked, smiling and laughing and blowing bigger and bigger puffs of cold air into the night. Luke opened the barn door and grabbed the lamp. But this time after he lit it he carried it outside and with Mary at his side took a much more careful look at the fresh snow. There were tracks, someone had been here, sled tracks.

But who would have left packages? For a quick moment, Luke thought that Mary had another suitor, maybe one she didn't even know about. But the thought passed as they followed the deep sled tracks. The tracks led to nowhere, they followed them back and they didn't have a starting point. It was as if the sled had come down out of the sky and left again, up and into the sky. Luke squatted and set the lamp on the snow, look here Mary, these aren't horse tracks or cow tracks, they look more like deer tracks, huge deer tracks. They're the only ones here, this sled was pulled by a bunch of deer, flying deer at that." Mary looked at Luke as they burst out laughing, they laughed until they hurt and thought they could laugh no more and then they sat down in the snow and laughed some more. They made snow Angels, threw handfuls of snow at each other and laughed until they were too cold and too worn out to laugh anymore.

Luke walked Mary to the house then went back to the bunkhouse and slept as soundly as he had in—well maybe it was the best sleep he'd ever had. He woke to the first rays of Christmas sunshine, coming from the east facing bunkhouse window, feeling refreshed and ready for anything and everything. Christmas day reminded Luke of his childhood, happy and carefree. The opening of the packages was both surprising and memorable. Mary's presents to the boys were wooden tops and puzzles and also a new shirt for each. Luke opened his gift from Mary, all the time feeling sorry that he didn't have something for her. Hard candy, she had made candy for him, he had eaten little of it since he was a kid but after one bite he knew he still had a taste for it—or maybe it was because of who made it, Luke was not sure." "Luke, it's time for the special packages, would you fetch them please and pass them out." Mary nodded to Luke as he gathered the four packages with the bright ribbons from under the small tree.

A new sewing basket complete with spools of thread, needles and thimbles for Mary a shiny black *Bible* for Luke and new shoes and rubber balls for the boys. Now it was even more of a puzzle, the shoes fit each boy perfectly.

Never another word was spoken about the mystery gifts on that first Christmas together, Mary and Luke spent many more happy Christmas days together. Fifty-one to be exact, they were married the Sunday after Christmas and lived happily ever after.

~6~
In The Year of the Lord, 1881

George Riley slid his pickup to a stop and stumbled through the door. He hadn't been drinking, just tired. Another day and he felt done in. Every day in the factory, where he was a foreman, seemed longer that the day before and every week was endless. Must be age, he thought, old age setting in, then he smiled despite how he felt, he was 26. George stared into the refrigerator trying to decide between leftover pizza, from two nights ago, or the Chinese from last night. He settled for the Chinese, waited the 90 seconds for the microwave to finish, grabbed the steaming bowl and walked into his bedroom. He sat on the edge of the bed and turned on the TV.

He hit the Netflix button and searched Christmas movies, scrolling through dozens of titles, most he had never heard of. Then he found the movie he wanted, his all-time favorite Christmas movie, *A Miracle on 34th Street*. Actually he had long had affection for two Christmas stories this one and his favorite writer Charles Dickens's classic, *A Christmas Carol*. Tonight he was tired and felt more like watching Santa Clause than Ebenezer Scrooge.

George hadn't watched a Christmas movie this year, hadn't been in the mood. Seemed he spent most of his off hours watching TV reruns of old westerns and detective shows. That was the extent of his life, other than work and lately that was mostly a drag.

George finished his late supper tossed the bowl in the trashcan and got ready for bed. He picked up the remote to turn off the movie, but it was pretty good, he let it go but fell asleep before much had happened.

But this time the sleep was short and not filled with dreams of Christmas past, only a quick view of his ex-wife, the one where she carried two suitcases from their apartment and left, left after 20 dreadful months together.

An hour later the movie was over and the TV was playing one of the Michael J. Fox, *Back to the Future*, movies. He thought for a moment that it might be fun to go forward to the future, then changed his mind deciding it would be more fun to go back in time.

This time he slept soundly for two hours, possibly a bit more. When he awoke, he was not sure where he was, the past, future – didn't look like it was the present, at least he didn't think so.

He wasn't sure why, but instead of looking around or taking a peek out the front door he went over to the fireplace, one that was not part of his small apartment a few hours ago, and tossed two large logs from a stack near the fireplace on the still warm coals. Then he looked outside. He gasped, it was dark, too dark, no lights, no lights anywhere, except for stars and a clouded crescent moon. Snow stood deep and the moon outlined a building fifty or so yards away, some kind of barn or shed.

A muffled noise near the rear of the house turned him around and he walked down a narrow hall and opened the first door. A bedroom with a pair of small beds and two soundly sleeping girls, they looked to be two or three years old. A little lamp burned in the corner casting an eerie yellow light on the sleeping girls. Ben took his time extinguishing the light, closed the door, stepped out and opened the door across the hall.

"Bedtime honey," said the beautiful woman tucked under the covers reading a book by lamplight.

Ben stumbled backward through the door, not knowing if he should thank his lucky stars and jump in bed or run for his life. He did neither. Instead, he went to the kitchen lit a candle and sat down at the hand-hewn table. He may have been in shock, he really was not sure. Deciding he needed a Tylenol or a hand full of ibuprofen he headed down the hall toward the bathroom, realized there was no bathroom and returned to the front room.

He thought for a few minutes about sitting down in his chair again and dreaming himself back into his old world. Then he thought, why. It was not a very satisfying world maybe he would stay in this one. He had a lot to think about.

Remembering he'd left the candle burning in the kitchen he returned to put it out, funny he didn't recall the paper under the candle. He slipped the paper from under the candle, turned it over and read.

"Sometimes you get what you need - not what you ask for," It was signed,

Santa

Year of the Lord, 1881.

Ben picked up the candle and walked out the front door. He could see tracks, looked like sled tracks and small hoof prints, tiny ones, must have been six or eight. He stepped back inside, checked the fire, walked down the hall, opened the door, the second one, and crawled into bed.

And like all good Christmas stories they all lived happily ever after.

~7~
Sleigh Bells Ring

And all the bells on earth shall ring,
On Christmas Day, on Christmas Day,
Then let us all rejoice again!
On Christmas Day in the morning.
(Traditional anonymous)

Harding Fielder felt like better days must be coming because today was miserable. If he made it home every day, the rest of his life should be better than this one. Didn't seem like such a big task three days ago when he started. He'd told Maude. "Four days, no longer, be back in four, easy," and he believed it.

When he said four days, he knew he was pushing, but they agreed he needed to be home within four days, because it was the twentieth of December, if he left first thing the next morning he would be home on Christmas Eve. Back carrying Christmas presents, and that was important to him. The kids had no presents last year and he'd bought nothing for his wife in two years. If anyone ever deserved a present at Christmas it was Maude, she was a saint putting up with their struggles and never complaining.

Starting the ride home the cold hadn't mattered, the ground was swept clean by the biting Wyoming wind and if he kept moving he could stay warm, almost. But three hours out of Fort Laramie the snow rode in from the west. A huge gray and black cloud obscured the sky, Harding knew, he had lived out here for years, this was bad.

Four days ago he couldn't believe his luck when the rider arrived with the note from Fort Laramie. Never a big rancher; some would say he wasn't much of rancher at all, but he'd been building up the place. Then, two years ago, the bad winter came, his herd was growing again but the process was slow and money was short. Scouting for the troopers out of the fort paid some every year and now with the Indian troubles lessening, work was scarce. Scouting for the fort might be paying off now in a different way, they needed beef and he was close enough to supply the troops.

Looked to Harding like he wasn't the only rancher having troubles, someone couldn't fulfill their government contract and the fort was running low on meat. It was tough to give up on this much beef, he really only had seven steers ready to sell, but the army said they needed a dozen or fifteen head and would pay top dollar.

By mixing in a couple of young bulls and some old cows, he put together a nice mix of beef for the fort. The ranch was going to make a payment to him and the family this year.

Getting the small herd to the fort two days ago now looked like the easy part. He tried to look to his side, eyes avoiding the ice and snow coming out of the west in bucketful's, wind driven and angry. Harding pulled his coat up higher and his hat down lower, wasn't likely the day would get any better.

Everything had gone so well at the fort. Top dollar for his beef, even the older cows he sold to make numbers match what they needed. If they'd have included ol' Moss in the sale, it would have been perfect. But there was a reason he called the cow ol' Moss, she was old, how old, he had no idea, best guess around fifteen or so. She stood still most of the time and laid down more than most cows. Harding was sure she'd soon have moss growing on her for lack of movement. The old cow hadn't had a calf since the kids were born, at least six years. He just never parted with her, first because she was a good cow that dropped good caves, made it through the blizzard and then she just got too darned old to sell. He hoped maybe the army was desperate. Took a half day extra with her in the bunch he drove to the fort. One look at the herd and the procurement officer said, "We'll take um all, all but that old mossy back, top dollar for the rest."

Harding turned his young gelding from west to north following the big bend in the North Platte. The strong west wind felt better to his side than it had in his face. For the first time today he believed he might make it. The past two hours, with every step, he supposed that he was going to freeze, not to be found until spring. About a half hour back, he daydreamed of giving up. But the bells calmed him, he might make it.

The snow came harder, the Wyoming sage turning to a blank white canvas. But he could still hear the bells. A snap purchase, something he rarely did, but he'd bought the sleigh bells on an impulse. Went back into the Sutler's store and paid another dollar for them. Then because it was the Christmas season, and he had nowhere else to put them, he'd tied them around ol' Mossy's neck. She looked pretty happy, had a new bounce in her step as she jingled along. The snow blinded him, the bells reassured him, at least he knew the old cow was still with him.

Near as he could figure he was within three or four miles of home. On a good day, he was only an hour and a half out, even with the rough terrain. The snow made everything difficult, his judgment of how fast he was traveling was uncertain, but his horse plodded through deeper and deeper snow. The wind intensified and the cold was worse than anything he had encountered in his life. Even the great blizzard of two years ago was not this bad. But when that blizzard hit he was home, not on a high Platte River ridge trying to get there. He ached all over, his gelding stumbled, and Harding knew neither he nor the horse had much left.

The bells were getting further and further away, the cow had wandered off. No need to go after her, she would make it home, starve or freeze out here, didn't matter, not anymore. Then he remembered the bells, didn't want to lose them. Against his better judgment, he turned toward the sound of the bells. It didn't take long to find her, or to at least find the sound, a minute, maybe a minute and a half. The bells sounded close, he felt like he could reach out and touch the old cow. After the quick pursuit, Harding was no longer sure which way was north and he needed to go north. The wind had turned again, or he had ridden a circle. The stinging wind, full of giant snowflakes and tiny ice crystals came from his right, not his left. An east wind instead of west, east winds sometimes brought in storms, but he'd never seen one turn in a matter of one or two minutes, not during a storm.

The wind roared, the cold numbed him and the snow blinded him. Maybe a few more minutes, the horse stumbled again; neither had more than a few moments left. Harding used the only sense he had left and felt the saddle bags. Cans of peaches and two bolts of cloth, a bright blue and a pink with a pattern, the store clerk said that one was, "all the rage this year."

The other saddlebag held candy, a fancy rag doll and a harmonica, presents for the kids. This was going to be the best Christmas ever, but now...

The ol' mossy cow was going the wrong way, again. She'd turned, trying to walk away from the storm instead of into it. Wrong, Harding was sure of it, but he didn't bet his life on it, he followed the bells. The snow seemed to let up, Harding thought he saw a star high in the sky, the same way Mossy was walking. Harding knew nothing of stars. He knew he was dying, freezing, despite the difficulties he smiled. Smiled as he died, smiled because he knew nothing of stars, directions or senile old cows.

The cow was moving slowly, Harding dismounted, knowing his horse was done in, maybe more than he was. They stumbled for what felt to be a quarter of an hour, not much more. Always following the bells, she'd know the way, instinct would take them home. He reached out, through the blinding snow, to put his hand on the cows back but couldn't find it. The bells were so close he reached again, still nothing. Then he decided the cow must be fifteen or twenty feet away from him, further than she sounded, the raging wind and blowing snow muffled sound and blinded vision, but she was there. The bells were clear, odd how clear they were with every other sound whistled away by the wind.

Harding crashed belly to rail and fell to his knees, the coral. His air escaped him and he wasn't sure if he could get up. He rolled to his knees and pulled himself up shaking and shivering. He felt around the rails, walked into the barn and was overcome with warmth and fell again. This time from either joy or sheer exhaustion, he was going to live.

It was Christmas afternoon before he woke up, tired, sore, hungry but otherwise, looked like he would be all right. Harding wasn't sure if he had walked into the house or someone carried him, didn't matter. But he was in bed and warm and he could hear the family talking and laughing in the kitchen. And he could smell heaven, a peach pie in the oven.

After a most memorable Christmas Day, marred only by the squawking harmonica playing of his son, Harding was sure it was everything he'd dreamed of, the best ever.

Early the next morning, he walked and dug his way through the snow to the barn, his horse was fine, the saddle put up. He needed to check on the cows. He had put them in the back corral before he left for the fort so the wife and kids could watch after them in the rare case that a northerner would come in. They were all there and in good shape, all there, all there but ol' mossy, she wasn't there and she never came back.

It was late spring before Harding felt strong enough to make another trip to the fort. He found the remains of that old cow. Not much left of her by then, nature and predators had done a job on her. But there she laid, that old gray cow, looked like she had a non-removable smile on, what was left of her face. But she was seven or eight miles from the ranch and that couldn't be. She was beside him seconds before he fell into the corral rail. Had she turned around and went back? Where were the bells, they should be here? Harding spent most of an hour searching the area. Scrub brush, sand, and sage were sparse on the windswept high planes trail, the bells were gone. He doubted anyone had found them, not this early in the spring, not a soul had passed this way since the storm, except him, today.

When he bought them, Harding had plans for those bells. He wanted to hang them on the ranch house front door, so when anyone came in they would jingle. He always liked the way the bell rang when he entered the Sutler's store. Thought the sound would be a nice touch at home.

The rest of the ride was daydreaming and uneventful. When he reached the fort Harding strode into the store, he had questions. He exchanged smiles with the young lady clerking in the shop but no pleasantries, he had questions. "Remember the bells I bought just before Christmas, well I need some more, those didn't make it home, do you have any, or will you need to order them for me."

The young lady smiled again, and in a muffled laugh answered. "You sure do get right to the point, don't you Mr., Fielder? We did have some bells at Christmas, can order one for you if you like, which did you have, the big tin cowbell or the little glass hand ringer, they sure were nice, made in Italy, you know."

"The sleigh bells, the one with ten or twelve bells on a leather strap."

"Oh, that would be nice, but we never had any sleigh bells here, I saw some once when we were in St. Louis."

At the sound of the conversation the store owner came around from the back room and added, "Sleigh bells might be nice, think anyone other than you would want any, I could look and see if I can order a set if you like."

Harding mumbled something about later and left the store. The next morning he packed up his provisions, including a contract for twelve head the first of November, and rode north and west along the river, riding home.

The ride gave Harding much to think about and think he did. But he had no idea of what happened to the bells. Dusk arrived with a splash of gold, red, and sparkling orange, a sunset made for Wyoming. The air freshened but today there would be no trouble getting home, the sky was clear, darkness should bring a beautiful, clear evening. Then he heard the bells.

At first Harding thought maybe he dozed off in the saddle, and then he heard them again. He looked around, but there was nothing out there to see, but he could hear the clear sound of the bells close by. He followed the bells, followed until they rode him right into his coral.

Harding never heard the bells on the trail again. But sometimes on a clear winter night he stepped out on the front porch and looked up at the sky to a group of stars that looked like a big old cowboy's gap tooth smile with a single extra bright star right in the middle.

The sight never failed to make him smile, smile and remember and think, clear as a bell.

For the rest of his life, he walked out on the porch every Christmas Eve and looked at that bright star in the east, the Christmas Star, and if he listened very carefully, he thought he could hear the bells.

When they saw the star, they rejoiced exceedingly with great joy. **Matthew 2:10**

~8~
The Kind of Guy He Was

The old cowboy rode along at a slow walk, he'd owned cars and trucks for more than 20 years, maybe time passed him by, he didn't care. It was 1952 and he remembered a time before automobiles, a slower, gentler time and then the wars, two big ones, changed everything. Something in the wind moved him back to 1952 again. He tipped his nose toward the sky and sniffed. It was wood smoke. A half hour back, before the wind freshened, he thought he smelled smoke but passed it off, thinking if old people could start seeing things and hearing things maybe he started smelling things that were not there. But now he was sure, it was smoke.

But that couldn't be, not in December, matter of fact it's the 24th, Christmas Eve. Good memories started to fill his head, but he pushed them away as quickly as they had come on. Christmas was just another day in December to him, nothing special, at least to him, not anymore.

People didn't camp this high up in December, hunting season was long past and the only house, except for his, five miles away, was the old Godfrey place. It was maybe three-quarters of a mile over the ridge to the north. The smell of burning wood was coming with the north wind, but that place had been vacant for what, 20 years, at least 15?

Clark Banks pulled up to think, but only for a moment, he had to know, that was the kind of guy he was. The sun was setting, it would be late when he got home, but he tapped his heels to the side his gray gelding and loped north picking his way through flat rocks and yucca.

He always liked the old Godfrey place, isolated, but picture perfect, like a bank calendar picture. The place set in a natural mountain park surrounded by junipers and berry bushes. Years ago when he and Bette last visited the Godfrey's they were old and frail and the place had been falling apart. Couldn't be much of anything left now.

Another minute and Clark Banks reached the crest of the hill that overlooked the long deserted place. Only three times in his 65 years had something left him speechless, the day he got married when their only child was born and now as he looked down on the old Godfrey place.

The Junipers were sparkling with thousands of multi-colored lights. The cabin he remembered as small and in complete disrepair was larger, much larger than he remembered. It was old but perfect, looked sound, complete with light showing through the windows. The smoke he'd smelled was from the cabin with the wind angling north pushing it from the chimney in great black and white billows. There was a large barn that hadn't been there 20 years ago along with half a dozen outbuildings and four large corrals.

Banks had not taken a drink of alcohol for years, right now he needed a drink, but he settled for a thorough rubbing of his eyes and another look at the scene below, a scene that did not change. He let the gray pick his way down the steep hillside, he had to see, he had to know, that's just the kind of guy he was.

A thought crossed his mind as he neared the twinkling cabin, what if this place is full of outlaws, escaped convicts or crazy people. This could be his last minute on earth, then he smiled at the lights twinkling as dollar sized snowflakes started to fall. If this is his last minute to live it would not be too bad. He warmed as the snowflakes splattered his face, chuckled to himself, and then laughed aloud, "don't think bad people decorate for Christmas," he said to the sagebrush and snow.

The old cowboy tied his horse to the rail in front of the cabin, stepped on the porch and the door opened as if he were expected. A white-bearded gentleman in a red vest smiled and motioned him in. Banks felt rather young looking at the old fellow, thinking, "This guy has me by at least 20 years."

"Can I get you something to warm ya up, Tea, Arbuckle's, whis"

"You have Arbuckle's, real Arbuckle's, haven't tasted that since before I went off to France in the first war, love some."

Banks watched the old man take a one pound bag of Arbuckle's Ariosa Blend from the cabinet and make coffee on the massive wood stove in the kitchen part of the cabin. It was good, better than anything the old cowboy had tasted in years, but how did he do it, Arbuckle's' hadn't made coffee, let alone Ariosa Blend for years.

The two men sat and talked for hours, talking about everything and chatting about nothing, like two old friends they talked into the dark of night.

When the old cowboy woke up, he could not remember falling asleep. Now he was stretched out on the couch, his boots beside him on the floor. He was toasty warm and he rolled back the red and green feather comforter and turned to get up. He was all alone. He thought the old man must be outside. Slipping on his boots he walked out on the porch, half a foot of snow covered everything in sight, his horse was gone, but he knew it was in the barn. He also knew he was all alone, he could feel things, just the kind of guy he was.

Banks went back into the house, he was hungry and he wanted to taste that

Arbuckle's one more time. A skillet of bacon sat on the stove, beside a pot of mush and a pot of coffee, and, of course, it would be Arbuckle's, he thought. Funny but he was sure there was nothing on the stove when he stepped outside, must have failing vision along with everything else in his old age. Then he felt it or didn't feel it, he had no aches and pains, the ones that had been with him since his army days. The coffee was good, but he wasn't sure it had magical healing powers.

It was time to go home, he wished he could say goodbye to the old timer, thought he might ride back up here in the spring. But now it was time to leave, he had things to do, and he felt different, happy and healthy. Walking to the barn it seemed almost warm, Banks considered for a moment that he might have stumbled upon a mountain valley style, fountain of youth.

Tracks near the barn stopped him, some kind of sleigh tracks, but the animals pulling it were not horses, smaller like deer tracks but larger, huge deer. He saddled the gelding and rode out of the barn right into the bright sunlight of his own place. How it happened, he did not know, but he was home.

Was it a dream, did he have a stroke and die, was he in heaven now? Nope, he was pretty sure his place would not do for heaven. Didn't matter, he had things to do.

Clark Banks rode to town in a gallop; it was early, old man Tatum would open the store for him, especially after he told him he intended to buy a present for every kid in town.

He wasn't sure why he had so much Christmas spirit, maybe it was just the kind of guy he was.

~9~

Four Magic Cookies and the CCC

Howie Fick and Philip Palmer, best friends and unemployed. This depression stuff they had been hearing about for the past few years did not mean much to these two. After all, they had been in high school doing what high schoolers do. Now they were graduates, the class of 1932, Middlebranch, Texas High School. They and 26 others were in the class and graduation was the typical exciting time for the two friends.

Now it was October, going on five months, and still, no jobs, and they weren't the only ones. More than three million Americans were out of work and most of them were looking for jobs. Howie and Philip knew their chances of finding employment were the old cliché, slim and none. So bad, that in lighter moments they often referred to each other as Slim and None. Philip, Slim, because he wasn't and Howie, None, because he never believed it. Howie continually thought the next place he looked he would find a job. It never happened.

October stretched into November and soon it was 1933. Still no jobs and no prospects for one. The first week of February Philip and Howie no longer wanted to burden their already cash-strapped families and they left town. Hopped a freight train and headed to the city. It took them less than one day in Dallas to understand times were tough everywhere, not just in tiny Middlebranch, Texas.

Ten days, and no work or money, the boys grabbed another flatcar rolling south. They spent more than a month looking for work and finding a day, or half day, here and there up and down the gulf coast. By the end of January the two were desperate and thought about going home, but knew that was a bad idea.

Christmas was more than a month past but to these two, homeless, broke teenagers it sure seemed like Christmas had arrived. Jobs, they had jobs. Until two days ago Philip and Howie didn't know that Franklin Roosevelt had been elected President and didn't care. Now they were elated, Roosevelt had talked Congress into something called the Civilian Conservation Corps and Howie Fick and Philip Palmer were newly enrolled. They had jobs they were members of the CCC. Planting trees in the wind-blown Texas Panhandle didn't seem like much, but it was.

The young men, as required, had most of the money they earned sent home. $25.00 each month went home and they kept $5.00, not much, but for Howie and Philip a near king's ransom.

The six months went by quickly and Howie and Philip immediately signed up for another six-month hitch. This time is was better, the job, not the pay. The pay was the same but now they were experienced workers and both became trail building crew foreman. Building trails for people to take recreational walks seemed an odd thing to be doing, but they enjoyed the work, often joking that it was very possible that not one single person would ever hike their trails.

This time, the two were not sure if they wanted to re-up for another six-month hitch. They talked late into the night about hitting the rails again, maybe to the west coast. California was hiring fruit pickers, or at least that was the talk among the men. California was warm and Howie was sure the wind could never blow as long, or as hard anywhere, as it did in Texas. Then something came up that changed their minds – a chance to move on. The two would still be with the CCC, but would be part of a startup crew moving to Wyoming. For two young men that had never been outside the boundaries of the state of Texas, this sounded like quite an adventure. They had no idea how wonderful the adventure would be, both wonderful and magical.

For many people, a two-day bus ride from Texas to Wyoming would be about as bad as it gets. Not for Howie and Philip, they looked out the windows at the passing scenery and joked and talked all the way. By the time their bus reached the Wyoming line everyone on board was in a great mood anticipating nothing but happiness and a terrific time when they reached the new camp.

Camp Bureau of Reclamation nine or BR-9, as it would be know was everything and more than the Texas men thought it would be. Their camp was in the heart of small mountains with a spectacular view of the North Platte River. They had never heard of the river, but it was stunning. A brand new dam backed up water for miles through deep canyons, cedar, pine trees, and huge boulders were everywhere. They had never seen anything like it.

Two weeks later 200 Texas workers were settled in, building roads and breaking trails. The mountain air set well with the young men and work moved at a rapid pace. August rolled around and this time re-enlisting was easy. CCC men could serve four hitches, two full years, Howie and Phillip decided, why not.

The two were now among the most experienced of all the CCC workers and found themselves as full-time supervisors, looking after mainly first time workers. They liked the work and were in constant wonder at Lakeshore Drive the long winding recreational road they were building along Lake Guernsey. Three weeks ago workers started to build a massive stone museum on the bluff above Camp-9 and at the foot of a mountain the workers called Round Top.

A beautiful fall turned to an early winter and the workers became more subdued and their moods grew somber. Howie and Phillip had seen this before, Christmas was approaching and the men longed for home. They couldn't go home, they knew that, but they wished times were better and they could be home again.

Howie constantly joked with the workers trying to lighten the mood and keep them happy. It wasn't working. The winds blew more each day and the nights became colder and colder. The work was tough now, BR-9 Commander Coffman, shortened the work day and extended the noon dinner hour, it helped but not much.

By the third week of December, the weather the work and the workers all turned miserable. A few men took off during the night a week ago and two more left last night, Times were tough, but home called and called louder and louder as the weather turned on the workers. If there was to be a saving grace for the men and the camp it came with the mail. When letters and the occasional packages from home arrived spirits lightened. The problem was that letters and packages were few, postage was money that didn't need to be spent from home. Most of the time the men were left without a word from home making mail call a time of repressed expectations instead of cheerfulness.

For Howie and Philip, mail call was no different, neither had a letter in the past few months. Then the package came, addressed to Howie Fick. He had no idea what it held and it didn't matter, it was from home. Howie took the package back to his bunk and unwrapped it slowly. It did not matter what was inside, it only mattered that it was from home. At first Howie felt bad for his best friend, who had not heard a word from home or family in more than a year. Phillip sat across the aisle on his bunk enjoying watching as Howie pulled the brown paper from the small box.

Four cookies with a note, he had heard from home. He sat the cookies aside and read the note, then said, "Hi," to Phillip because the short letter said he should.

"Magic Cookies," my mom says these are magic cookies," Howie said.

Phillip smiled and started to laugh, thought better of it and leaned back on his bunk to see what Howie would say next. Howie sure could be a joker. Howie snapped one of the cookies in half handed it to Phillip and said. "What if these were magic cookies like mom said, she said each cookie had one wish baked in. What should we wish for?"

Now, both boys laughed and Phillip said, "How about a couple of big ol' soft beds to replace these Army cots, and over in the corner where there's more room." They laughed again, broke one cookie in half, shared it, then sat the rest of the cookies aside, just in case, and headed out in the cold.

The afternoon was short, and the boys had a couple of hours to kill before supper. Howie opened the door to their sleeping dorm and stopped dead in his tracks. Phillip bumped into him then saw what had stopped Howie.

Their bunks, they were in the back, all alone. They were huge, and soft looking with blankets and pillows piled on each. Howie and Phillip needed to talk.

Relaxing was easy, but more than a bit embarrassing on their new spacious beds in the corner, but it was a good place to talk. "I can't believe it, these cookies really are magic, that's not possible, is it - magic?" Howie said.

Phillip tried to say something but couldn't. The two sat in silence for the next five minutes. At last Phillip said, "what you gonna do with the cookies, looks like you got three wishes coming, better be careful what you want."

An hour later the wishes were set, a million dollars for Howie and a million for Phillip that was wish one. A new, paid off, farm for each of their parents, that was wish number two. It took a while before they came up with number three but at last they decided on a new high school for Middlebranch Texas. Yep, the fighting Longhorns of Middlebranch High School, would have a new and modern home.

Howie put the three cookies in his foot locker deciding that he would make the wishes on Christmas Eve, still a few days away, that way it will be a special Christmas for their families.

It seemed to take forever but the 23rd day of December, at last, rolled around. In a few hours Howie, Phillip and their families would be set for life, and in a town with a terrific new high school. Life was good for the two young men of the Civilian Conservation Corps. Tomorrow they would eat the cookies make the wishes and head back home for Texas.

Things changed on the 24th. When Phillip awoke, Howie was gone, his bed had been slept in and made up. Phillip went on with his usual routine and for the first day in two years did not see his Howie. That night when Phillip went to bed, Howie was still nowhere to be seen. Phillip tossed and tumbled all night long, worrying and wondering about his best friend. Sometimes he thought he ran off and at other times he believed someone found out and had stolen the three magical cookies. At long last, the morning light filtered through the east windows. Phillip got out of bed and started the fifty-yard walk to the mess hall for breakfast, then he heard music.

Music and laughter, Phillip ran the rest of the way to the mess hall. Inside Howie was passing out letters, letters from home and there was one for everyone. In the front of the room was an enormous stack of packages, one for every man in Camp-9, Phillip knew right away what had happened, the cookies. Wishes had been made and wishes had been fulfilled.

Phillip laughed, despite himself, knowing he was not going to be a millionaire, not today anyway. He poured himself a cup of coffee and sat down to enjoy the sheer happiness of Christmas morning in Civilian Conservation Corps Camp-BR-9, Guernsey Wyoming. He took a handful of cookies and another of Christmas chocolates deciding to stuff himself, after all it was Christmas.

He wanted to ask, but he never did. Phillip never asked Howie why? One cookie for the letters from home, one for the presents and one for the endless pile of Christmas goodies. He didn't know where the 12 foot overly decorated tree fit in, but he didn't ask, maybe Howie found another cookie.

It took a few days, but life in the camp soon returned to normal. In March Howie and Phillip were mustered out of the CCC. Phillip went home to Texas, for a short time, but Howie never went back. Howie and Phillip were not destined to see each other again. Phillip went on to a distinguished journalism career and Howie disappeared.

At the national 50 year CCC reunion one former Camp-9 worker reported he knew what happened to Howie. Said he moved north, far north, all the way to the North Pole. He said

Howie was and had been, Santa Clause, for the past five decades.

And that is the magical story of How(ie) Santa Clause continues to deliver Christmas happiness, joy, and magic each and every year.

~10~

The Tall Stranger Ordered Eggnog

Finally, it was December and that meant Christmas was not far away. Christmas is a time for magical and wonderful happenings, magical and wonderful happenings everywhere.

The tall stranger bellied up to the bar at the Hartville Miners and Ranchers Saloon. He watched in the mirror as the patrons lowered their heads and moved back away from him. A wry smile turned the corners of his mouth bending it inside his drooping mustache. He dug with a cold hand in his coat pocket and pulled out a weathered dollar bill, straighten it a bit and pressed it on the counter.

He didn't say a word, he didn't need to, everyone knew what he wanted and everyone watched. It was cold outside, too cold even for December in Wyoming. The big man's right hand rose as if in slow motion, he grabbed his collar and in one smooth motion turned it down onto his shoulders. Swiping a big hand across his neck, crystal flakes of ice fluttered to the barroom floor. He unbuttoned his heavy coat, pulled it off, and carefully placed it on the empty bar stool to his right. He sat down on the stool staring straight ahead, saying nothing. A collective sigh came from the customers, those who had not sneaked out yet, as he sat down and all could see he was not packing the usual Colt 45 on his left hip. Now usual might be a stretch, as no one in the bar had ever seen him with a Colt, but the story, the one they had all heard, said he carried one, and could use it, and had, but not today.

It happened once every year, this man came to town, this town anyway, one time a year. As far as the other customers were concerned, once was enough, for most of them once was too often. This silent man was the tall, dark stranger that writers made up stories about, or worse, wrote true stories about. But he really was not tall and dark, not any longer. It was more like he once might have been tall and dark. Now he was rather round and white from age, mustache, beard and hair, but for some reason he scared the patrons in the bar. Seemed like when he came in the rough talk stopped and everyone was at once on their best behavior – odd.

The barkeep reached slowly, after first making eye contact he could not hold, under the counter and pulled out a clean mug, turned his back to the stranger and filled it from a brass pitcher perched atop the wood stove cornering the back bar. He carefully sat the still foaming mug in front of the tall stranger with the big thirst. Then he turned again reaching low under the counter, a glint of metal showed in his right hand. His hand came up quickly, but not too fast, and placed a large scoop of vanilla ice cream into the steaming mug of eggnog.

Why this bar, this town? He seemed to enjoy the fact that everyone appeared to be afraid of him, no one was sure why. The patrons filed out, one by one, and in a quarter of an hour the barkeep and the eggnog drinking mysterious man were the only two left. It took a bit of courage but after another few minutes the barman said, "So what brings you to town stranger?"

"Eggnog"

"That's it, I only see you once a year and that's it, just for the eggnog," the bartender said.

"Eggnog with a dip of vanilla ice cream," the stranger corrected.

The bartender, now feeling a bit more brave pressed on, "Where you from," he asked.

This time the stranger looked up and took a little time, ten seconds, maybe more, before answering, "Up North, from up north, quite a ways north." Then he took another long drink of the eggnog.

By now the bartender was starting to relax, maybe this stranger was not such a bad man after all. He wanted to ask another question but before he could, the mystery man rose to his feet, pulled his coat from the stool next to him, and headed for the door. Funny, the bartender thought, he'd never noticed those red suspenders before, thought he came in here wearing a black coat, not a red one.

"Hey mister, I don't see a horse, where's your horse?"

The stranger paused before pushing through the door then said, "Came in my sled, too much snow to get here from up north with a horse."

That made perfect sense to the barkeep, seemed the last few years more and more, ranchers especially appeared to be using sleds to get about in the winter. Ever since ol' Jim Lloyd invented the hay sled out at the big ranch it had become popular to replace buggy wheels with runners in the winter, quite the rage these days. Then a thought crossed the bartenders mind, no snow, hadn't seen a flake, not in the fall and not yet this winter, not a flake. He ran to the door pushed it open to holler at the stranger, wanted to ask how in the world he ran a sled on dirt, but he was gone.

Funny he thought, he shouldn't be more than a few steps away, but he had vanished.

"Oh well," the bartender said to the empty bar as he walked back past the vacated tables. Time to tidy up a bit anyway. He busied himself the next few minutes wiping off tables and pushing chairs back in place. Grabbing his broom from the corner he started to sweep up, deciding if no one else was coming in he might as well close up.

As he pushed the broom under the brass rail in front of the bar, he noticed a piece of green paper, a neatly folded piece of paper. Nothing odd about that, he found lots of things when he was cleaning up, sometimes money. But this time it was not money, green but not money. He picked up the paper, started to toss it toward the trash can but instead decided to open it. And what he saw, well what he saw was the real story.

Written in bold print at the top of the paper were these words, maybe it would be easier to just show you that little piece of green paper. If I don't you readers, none of you, will believe it so – here it is.

Final Naughty and Nice Report

Wyoming

Hartville Miners and Ranchers Saloon

Naughty – *no one, no not one*

Nice – *everyone, yes every single one*

This is always one of my favorite checkpoints. All the patrons seemed to be nice young fellows who went home to their families, where they belong, at a good time. I must look like a time reminder, or something because everyone seemed to leave when I went in for my, once a year, eggnog with a scope of vanilla.

S. Clause

North Pole

"We'll I'll be," the bartender said.

He grabbed his coat, locked the saloon door and began the two block walk to the boarding house he called home. He started to whistle then shouted, but not too loud, to anyone within earshot.

"Merry Christmas one and all, it's going to be a wonderful Christmas, wonderful indeed, Merry Christmas Hartville."

Then it started to snow, big delightful, magical flakes.

Mr. Dickens and the Christmas Miracle

Ben Dalton slammed the door, maybe harder than he needed. Another day, another, what, he thought.

Opening the refrigerator he grabbed a Diet Coke, not much of a stretch, since the only other things now cooling were catsup, mustard, grape jelly and something in a cheap plastic container, he couldn't remember what.

Ben walked the five or six steps to his ancient recliner, kicked off his shoes, and fell into the chair. He reached for the remote and clicked on the TV. Thursday night should be a football game or maybe an early-season NBA game he thought. Instead he settled for a Christmas movie, wasn't sure why. Seemed like Christmas movies every day lately. He tapped on his cell phone to check the date, makes sense, December 22, getting close.

The movie was his favorite, "A Christmas Carol," and it was the good one, the old one with Mervyn Jones playing Bob Cratchet in beautiful black and white on his $2,000 dollar flat screen.

He watched for 20 minutes, felt his eyelids droop and promptly fell asleep. What happened next is hard to believe. But Christmas was near and magical things happen at Christmas.

Seemed like an hour or more when Ben awoke, stretched, felt good, better than he could ever remember, better than he had felt for, well for years. He reached for the remote, time to shut off the TV and go to bed. His hand couldn't find the remote in the dark room, he turned his eyes toward the television and saw nothing but the dying red embers of a huge rubble stone fireplace, no TV.

The Diet Coke can was still on the table beside him, but everything else in the room had changed. The off-white walls were now brown, looked to be log, the once bare walls were covered with paintings, tapestries and intricate embroidery work.

Just like a Christmas movie, Ben knew he was dreaming, had to be a dream, but how could he be dreaming of a dream? What's next a ghost, Marley's ghost? Ben fell back into the hard-backed chair that used to be a recliner and stared at the tin coffee cup he thought once held Diet Coke. Not sure if he was awake or still dreaming, he quickly fell back asleep.

Ben dreamt of Christmas, his job at the feed store, cowboys, the old west, and miracles. This time when he awoke it was morning and sunshine streamed through the east window. He smelled coffee and something else, freshly baked bread. Hearing a rustling behind him, Ben turned to see a woman, about his age, tending a fire in a small black cook stove. "Well, good morning sleepy, you must of wore yourself out yesterday," she said.

Ben had seen some strange things in his day, but this day, well, this day seemed to be taking him somewhere he had never been. Then he heard the kids, yes kids. More than one voice. He stood and turned, looking around the cabin as two youngsters pulled up chairs to the split log table in the kitchen.

He wasn't sure why he said it, but he looked at the children, who might have been eight or nine years old, maybe ten, and said, "Don't you kids have school today, you're gonna be late?"

The taller of the two, the girl, looked at Ben and answered, "Oh Papa, we don't have school today, it's Saturday, and tomorrow is Christmas Eve anyway, no school all next week, Christmas vacation."

Ben was more than a bit taken back, but it was all starting to make sense. He nodded and smiled, then said, "I believe you two are correct, that means today we cut a tree, a Christmas tree."

The house was silent, three faces looking at Ben. He wasn't sure how he knew, but instinctively he knew what was wrong. "I know we haven't had a tree before, but thought it was time, from this year on we will celebrate Christmas, every year, – enough talk, finish up you breakfast so we can go cut a Cedar."

Ben felt her arms stretch around him from behind, then she pulled him tight kissing him lightly on the back of his neck, "Thanks, Ben," she said.

Ben turned and pulled her toward him and said, "That's all right Louise, it was time." Then he squeezed her tight wondering how he knew her name.

The family of four went together, found and cut a tree and spent most of the rest of the forenoon and part of the afternoon making decorations and hanging them on the tree.

The next morning Ben read the Christmas story from the *Bible,* explaining with his own interpretations as he read. Including his rather strange reasoning for reading the story from the book of Mathew on the 24th instead of Christmas day. He described to them how it took the wise men a long time to reach Bethlehem so he wanted to give them some time to think about the Christmas story before Christmas day because that wasn't such a long time. The three listeners didn't question his reasoning, but even Ben thought his own explanations sounded a little odd. He wasn't ready, not yet, to tell them about his Christmas morning surprise.

Ben, Louise, and the kids were up before the sun on Christmas morning. Louise had already built a fire in the cook stove and a pot of apple cider simmered, giving the cabin an aroma that was unmatched in Ben's memory. Now it was time for Ben's treat, no not the presents, not yet.

While doing chores, yesterday morning, Ben had found a small book wrapped in brown paper in the barn. That might have been surprising if not for all the other strange goings on in the past few days. Most strange of all might be that he knew what chores to do and how to do them. He knew that he was married to Louise and that he had two children, Davy, and Betsy.

The book he found, *A Christmas Carol*, was by Charles Dickens. Ben read four different selections, then pronounced himself done an hour after starting his now familiar, to the family, reading and explaining.

His family didn't ask where the book came from and he did not offer any information. Nor did he offer information on the presents, the first ever opened in their home. The presents he found in the hay loft, wrapped in old burlap. Each was tagged and covered in colorful paper, there was even one for him.

The days and then the years passed by and Ben thought less and less about his old life. As a matter of fact, he was not sure there was an old life. Might have been a dream, a vivid dream. He vaguely remembered watching pictures, pictures moving and talking on a wall and remembered or thought he remembered something of a house, not made of log, but he remembered little else. Sometimes he wished he could remember if he had a job in his other life or in his dream life. Since he couldn't remember Ben decided he must not have had a job, or he had one, he would rather forget.

Ben Dalton grew old, his wife ever by his side. The kids grew and then the grandkids had families of their own. Ben and Louise were both a year past 80 when the Christmas season again rolled around. It was still a big affair in the Dalton home, as it had been for fifty years. But this one would be different, he could feel it, perhaps it was his old bones creaking in the cold.

Early on the morning of the 24th of December and long before the family was to gather for Ben's reading from the book of Matthew. Ben walked from the fire he had built to the kitchen table and sat down across from his wife.

"Louise, I've had this feeling, maybe it was a dream, for so long and I need to talk to you about it, wanted to for a long time but didn't know how to start. Just never understood, never did, maybe you can make some kind of sense out of it."

Louise walked over to a small shelf, high up on the wall opposite the fireplace and pulled from the half dozen books they owned their copy of, *A Christmas Carol,* and handed it to Ben. Louise dabbed at tears in her eyes and said, "You mean the dream that started with this story?"

Ben was astounded and for the moment speechless. "You knew, how did you know about the dream?" he said.

"Oh, it was not a dream Ben, it was real. Real Christmas magic. The book holds the magic. It came all the way from England and is signed by Mr. Dickens himself, signed with his own hand. He needed money badly, he was broke and down on his luck. He was afraid no one would buy, *A Christmas Carol,* with a ghost of all things, or any of his other books. Thought he was done as a writer. That's why he took the first five books from the printer home. He laid his hand on each one and prayed for a miracle before signing and then wished for Christmas magic. He needed to sell books, needed a miracle and it happened, he sold books, many of them. This book is one of the five, one of the five miracle books. Mr. Dickens willed these books to be magical."

Ben, for the second time in a few minutes, was speechless. He swallowed twice, stood up and walked a circle around the cabin. At last he said, "So it's real, I had another life, a life I can remember almost nothing of? I always thought it might be, real that is. But, where did the book come from?"

Ben waited for Louise's answer, an answer Ben thought he already knew. "Mr. Dickens gave it to me, handed it to me on a London street corner in 1843. I was broke with two little ones and at my wit's end. He handed it to me and said that he hoped it would bring me a little luck. The rest, well the rest is our story, Ben.

That evening Ben read from the good-book and the next day he read, with even more enthusiasm than usual, from Mr. Dickens.

~12~
The Mix Up

Dale Stephens pulled his color up in a failed attempt to shut out some of the cold wind. He rode down a steep sage filled draw, then paused before turning back into the wind. Winter days were getting tougher and tougher on him and now that he had turned 30 he guessed age was making the cold worse than it was. He stopped at a broken post and spent the next few minutes trying to wedge sticks in the hole and keep the post upright. Didn't look too bad, he thought, should be all right until spring when he could dig a new post hole and put in a proper post.

He'd been working on the same ranch, for old man Powell, J.L. Powell, since the day he turned 15. Half his life. Then he wondered how much longer it could last. He didn't want to change jobs, didn't want to move to town, and wasn't sure if he could, even if he had too. Working someone else's land was all he knew and all he wanted. Oh, sometimes he wished he was married, maybe had a couple of kids, but didn't look likely it would ever happen. Dale had never been serious about a woman in his life, never dated and had spent precious little time even talking to any women. Except that he did talk with J.L.s spinster daughter, Annie, once in a while.

Sometimes he daydreamed about marrying up with Annie, spinster or not, she wasn't that old, he remembered the big shindig Ol' J. L. threw for her 18th birthday and that was only seven or eight years ago. He talked to her some, just last week he'd asked if she needed help carrying stuff from the wagon into the house. She said, "Thanks, I can get it."

He rode out on the point, a natural stone outcropping with the best view on the ranch. Despite the cold, he crawled down from his horse and walked closer to the edge to take a long look. It was almost Christmas. He liked Christmas, didn't do anything different for it, but he liked it. His mind wandered and he thought about his lonely life. He lived by himself in the bunkhouse as he was J.L.s only hired man and had been for the last six years. The ranch furnished his food, which he cooked on an ancient iron stove near the front of the bunkhouse, horses, sleeping accommodations, and $60 dollars a month.

At times like this Dale often contemplated life and today he thought about the job. It was 1903 a new century, maybe there won't be any more Cowboys someday. The trail drive days were over and the old west he read about each evening was gone. He suspected it never really was, not with all the gunfights, bank robberies and all.

Then the loneliness hit him, it didn't often happen but getting close to Christmas he wished he had a family to share it with. He did have dinner every Christmas with J.L. and Annie, but that is not what he thought about. He missed having a family but knew he never would. The melancholy passed as quickly as it had arrived. Dale remounted and headed straight into the biting north wind. Riding toward the bunkhouse, another work day completed.

After coffee, beans, and biscuits, he pulled a book from the self, one that he only read at this time of year. It was one of his favorites, a book of Christmas short stories. One of the characters in his favorite story reminded him a bit of himself. A loner, who yearned for more in life, but never the less enjoyed life and wasn't sure if he could change. The loner, in this case, a sailor, wrote out a heartfelt story about how lonely he was. He slipped the paper into an old wine bottle, corked it, and tossed it into the sea a few miles from some mystical harbor. Like all great stories at Christmas must, this one had a happy ending. The message was found by a lonely young woman on Christmas Day, they met, got married and lived happily ever after.

Dale yawned, put a marker in the book, blew out his kerosene lamp, pulled the covers up and promptly fell asleep. The dim light of morning came with howling winds and blowing snow. It was Sunday, his day off, his only day off each week. Dale blew out a soft whistle of relief, tossed a few pieces of kindling into the potbellied stove and sat down in his rocker. A nice day to stay in.

Opening his book to the marker Dale started to read, then put the book back and took his small ledger book from his coat pocket, whittled a point on his pencil and started to write.

Dear Santa,

I know you are not real but if this letter makes me feel some better, then it will seem that you are real.

I have been told that you can bring about special presents, miracles, and wishes during the Christmas season. I hope it's true because my wish is a whopper.

My life is a good one, but it sure would be better if I was a married man, had my own family. Been thinkin' about it some lately.

117

I have a fine job that I like but miss not having a family. Not sure if anyone would have this old cowboy, but if they did I would be good to them. With your magic, I'm sure you know that I been in love with Annie, here at the ranch, for more years than I care to admit, but I know she is out of my class. Can you help me out?

Oh, and I cook pretty good too.

Sincerely,

A Lonely Cowboy – *Dale Stephens*

Satisfied he folded the note in a homemade envelope and sealed it with red wax. The note was not going to be mailed, where would he send it? The North Pole?

Dale walked to the barn, found an empty witch-hazel bottle, stuck the note inside, found the old cork, crammed it in, and put the bottle on top of a row of shelves. At that moment, he decided that he would toss the bottle in the creek when spring came. Let it wash downstream, see what happened. He felt better and walked back to his bunk whistling a Christmas song. Then started to sing softly, "*It came upon a midnight clear that glorious song of old.*"

He looked around, quickened his pace, bounded up the two steps to the bunkhouse opened the door and closed it behind him. He peaked out through the window and was relieved to see no one was about.

Annie Powell was about as close to being depressed as she had ever been. Annie was tired of being called J.L.s spinster daughter, after all she was only 27. She had always been shy, painfully so. She thought back to last week when their handsome hired man asked if she needed help carrying packages in the house. She did, but him talking to her embarrassed her and she'd said, "Thanks, I can get it."

How stupid, but that is what Annie always did when men talked to her, she became flustered and tongue tied. And it especially happened when she spoke to their hired man. She had no idea why, the two had known each other for, well it seemed like forever since she was a kid. He seemed as shy and lonely as her but Annie guessed he wasn't.

Now it was almost Christmas, and she wanted a present, not just any present, she wanted a husband. She couldn't decide if she should laugh at that thought, or not, since she had started to cry. Her shyness would keep her a spinster, the people were right, she would be a spinster forever.

Then she did something that surprised even her. Annie decided to write a letter to Santa. She knew he wasn't real, but suddenly felt like it might raise her spirits, talk to a man, even if he was make believe, one who worked with elves and owned flying reindeer. She took a piece of her special stationary, the paper she used to write, once each year, to her mother. Oh, how she missed her. Annie had only been 13 when her mother died and each year, on her mother's birthday, she wrote her a letter. All the letters were saved and stacked in her top desk drawer.

Tonight she would write her first ever letter to Santa and her first with the special stationery to someone other than her mother. When she was finished, it would be placed on the stack of letters to her mother. Then she changed her mind, not about the letter, but what she would do with it. Maybe she should mail it to the North Pole. Annie smiled, opened her bottle of ink, dipped the pen, and began to write.

Dear Santa,

This may be more than even you and your magic can do. You see, I am lonely and afraid I may grow old, and gray before my time. Life on the ranch with my dad is fulfilling and enjoyable but the last few years I have been having feelings that I am missing out on something. I want and, now I know, I need a family of my own. Not sure how or if you could ever make anything like that happen but if you could . . . . .

Annie didn't sign it, she never finished it. She was stuck. A half hour later she wrote the words she knew she had to write.

"I am in love with our hired man, have been for years, don't think he notices me much. Help me Santa!

Love

Annie

And thanks

Annie folded the note and laid it on her desk with no idea of what to do with it. She nearly laughed at herself for writing that silly letter and thought for a moment about destroying it. Instead, she let it be. She blew out her lamp and climbed into bed.

The next morning, for reasons she wasn't even sure of, Annie took the note to the barn with the idea of finding a bottle suitable to float her note in the nearby river. She took the first bottle that looked seaworthy and worked hard to remove the cork. She carefully rolled the letter and started to push it in the bottle. Then she saw it. Something was in the bottle blocking the way. She found a horseshoe nail and worked the small piece of paper out. It was the letter to Santa from Dale.

Annie took, but a few seconds to know what she was reading. A huge smile crossed her face, then she felt the heat that came with embarrassment. With tears lining her face, Annie knew she couldn't tell Dale. Funny, she'd never called him by his first name, not in all the years they had known each other. No, she could never tell him that she read the note. Carefully she dropped her note into the bottle, she wasn't sure why and tucked Dale's note into her jacket pocket. She walked back to the house humming a Christmas tune, a smile on her face she could not remove. Then for the first time in several years she started to sing. *"It came upon a Midnight clear, that glorious song of old."*

She started to turn and look around, see if anyone had heard her, then she decided it didn't matter, she smiled again and kept walking.

A few minutes after eating a quick lunch Dale, full of questions about himself, decided he needed to burn the note he'd written to Santa.

Burn it and continue with his lonely lifestyle. It didn't take much thinking, no one would have him – nothing but an old cowboy.

Grabbing the bottle from the shelf, harder than he needed, he pulled the cork free and shook the letter into his hand. Right away he could see it was not the piece of lined paper he had used. At first he thought maybe Santa changed something, then thought, no probably not.

He rolled the note open, sat down on a three-legged stool and read the letter, then read it again and a third time. He was stunned. Stunned, and like Annie, embarrassed, so much that he contemplated staying in the barn the rest of the day. Then thought for a moment about staying there for the rest of his life.

Annie knew she needed to talk with Dale. They had feelings for each other, maybe love. But she couldn't do it. She spent the day in her room, brooding and thinking.

Dale strode from the barn after much thought, he had expected to be there longer, but had only sat there for half an hour. That is all it took to sort things out. He walked toward the big house and there she was coming down the steps, walking toward him. They stopped three feet apart, said a few words to each other then started to laugh. In another minute they were hugging each other and ten minutes later the two new lovers sat on the porch holding hands.

They talked for more than an hour but stopped immediately when J.L. Powell, Annie's father, walked out through the front door. He saw the two, smiled and said, "Well it's about time, thought you two oddballs might never find each other, glad to see it, glad to see it."

Both Dale and Annie started to speak but stopped when J.L. held up his hand. "This is the funniest thing ever, I been wondering if the two of you would ever find each other, but didn't want to be a meddling old man so I never said anything. This year it was gettin' so worrisome to me I even sat down and penned a letter to Santa. Old man's fantasy, I asked him to get the two of you together. Not sure what I would have ever done with the thing, thought about givin' it to one of you, then decided maybe I'd bottle it and toss it in the river. Not sure the river runs all the way to the North Pole, though," then he chuckled and added, "Maybe I would have just sat you two down and read it to you."

Dale and Annie were married on Christmas morning, deciding, "Why wait." J.L. packed up and moved to town the next week. And as all good tales must end – they all lived happily ever after.

~13~
The Best Seller

Herb Allison cranked the weather-beaten wheel on his ancient John Deere hard to the left. The close-set front wheels pushed the soft sand out of the way as the tractor slid into the drive. Home, didn't look like much to others, but it did to him, he was home. Herb Allison had lived in this house since the day he was close enough to having it finished to move in. Built it himself, every brick and every stick of wood. He lived in the house for the better part of three years before it was completed, and now it had been 60 years in that house.

The barn, chicken house, and corral had all came later, and like the house, they were showing their age. No one noticed the barn and chicken house never had animals in them. Herb had long meant to get a few cows and some chickens but his was a busy life and animals took time.

Seems like he just woke up and went to work every morning with every next day being the same as every yesterday. Now he was 87 years old. Where did the years go?

He knew where the early years went, how could he have been born in 1928? Didn't seem that long ago, but to most it was. Ten years of his life made him the ancient, hardworking, near hermit that he appeared to be today.

Herb had loved high school, graduating with the exceptional class of 1946. The war ended with his school days and high-school graduate Herb Allison was ready for the world. He did okay in his classes, excelled at sports and stayed involved in the most popular clubs. He had girlfriends, an old Chevrolet jalopy and a part time job in Albert Jensen's grocery store. When he graduated, he tried college for a year, found it less than what he wanted and joined the Army.

Three years later he'd served his hitch and was ready for civilian life. He moved back home, fell in love and married. The next five years were now a blurred disaster. Divorce, a six-week job making cardboard in a box factory and he hit the road. Grabbed a flat car on a Rock Island Train and was gone. He didn't embrace the hobo life, he only needed a ride out of town.

When he reached Chicago, he jumped off and stayed. Found a clerking job in a small drug store and went to work. That's when he wrote the book, only one book. He wrote for hours every evening after work. Just one book, but it made him famous.

Not really famous as a person, he continued to live in the small apartment and kept his job for another year. All the while the book gained worldwide fame. No, Herb was not famous, it was the book, Herb's book that became famous. *A Disappointed Life*, his one, and only book became a worldwide sensation and an American Classic.

The book was a tragedy of life, sad but somehow it had broad appeal, first in America and two years later in Europe. Within a decade, the book could be found all over the world, translated into more than 60 languages. Herb read it once, as his own copy editor, sent it to a New York Publisher and forgot about it. He was genuinely surprised when they called, told him they loved it, and wanted to publish. The money surprised him even more. A man writing a book about how terrible life was and then the book made his life comfortable. At least his financial life.

A year later Herb Allison went back to the farm and disappeared, not in actuality, but in spirit. It all seemed so long ago to Herb, too long, a lifetime.

Herb crawled down from the tractor and started a slow painful walk to the back door of his house. He wasn't sure why he looked around every time he crawled down off the tractor, but he did. Pride, he guessed, didn't want anyone to see how stoved up he had become over the years. These days it took at least a full minute to crawl down and another half minute to straighten up before he could walk to the back door. He didn't want anyone to see him struggle with such a simple chore. But no one was watching, he hadn't had a visitor in nearly two decades. He went to town when he needed to, exchanged pleasantries with those who spoke first, but mostly kept to himself. He allowed himself a look toward town. The Christmas lights pleased him, always bright and cheerful, unlike the life he'd written about so long ago.

Herb had given money, anonymously, for the Christmas lights each year for the past three or four decades. Sometimes as much as $20,000 all to keep the Christmas spirit alive in his little town. All checks, like the first, were sent from his New York investor's office. Now it was time to give it away, all of it. Give the money away and die, that's what Herb had left. He reached up and ripped November from the calendar, it was already two or three weeks into December, he wasn't sure of the day. He turned on the radio to get the forecast and the date. December 21st, perfect. He didn't want his donations to be a big deal. It was so close to Christmas he knew the time was right. He didn't believe anyone would notice. He called his attorney in Chicago and gave his directions, "Give it away, all of it, before the 23rd." Herb died the next day, Christmas Eve day.

Herb Allison was mostly unknown, but he wasn't some scary guy who lived in the haunted farmhouse either. People liked him but didn't know him, he was mostly invisible. People in the area thought he was a good farmer, a very good farmer. Neighbors and townspeople had long speculated on the fact he might be a millionaire. Living alone and carrying on such a frugal life with all that old equipment. People were sure he must have paid off everything on the farm long ago. But Herb Allison was not a millionaire when he died his lawyers took their commission and gave away the rest, 1.4 billion dollars.

The city was shocked, especially the banker who thought him only a long time, well to do, bachelor farmer. His farming money was substantial, nearly two and a half million. Two and a half million he kept in the local bank.

But it was his story that shocked America, his untold story. Herb Allison had given away millions. An average of nearly ten million dollars a year for more than 50 years and it all started with a book, a book about life's disappointments. Every year his donations went out in the fall closer to Christmas, he liked it that way. Millions went to universities, small colleges, libraries, relief efforts, orphanages, all of the local churches, and many individuals who needed help. In a few cases, he sent money to help countries, most people had never heard of, to stave off financial collapse.

Herb Allison, the writer, had fans, fans he never knew and never embraced, but they were there. Ten thousand people lined the streets the day of his funeral. Newspapers, news magazines, and online writers published thousands of stories, all about the people he had helped, lives he saved. Instead of going away after the funeral, the stories were still going strong three months later and that's when his Chicago lawyer dropped the bombshell. There is another book.

Herb's story filled 19 spiral notebooks, written over several decades. It wasn't a diary it was a story, the story of his life. The last page said it all, Herb wrote it three weeks before he died. In bold print it said, "I finally have a title, *Self-Realization, and a Fulfilled Life*." The book was incredible, Herb loved his life, loved every day of it. He was not the lonely old hermit farmer his neighbors and locals thought he was.

The reason Herb never raised livestock was simple, he didn't stay on the farm year round. Each year when the harvest was over he left. The locals didn't miss him, most didn't know he wasn't around. He visited Chicago, New York, and Los Angles on business and traveled widely for pleasure. He attended Broadway shows and the opera, always with a lovely lady at his side.

And he wrote Christmas stories, thousands of them, under two dozen different names and published them all. In New York, Chicago and L.A. he was the reclusive mystery man, a celebrity in name only, the celebrity that no one knew. When he was in their midst, they hobnobbed with him but had no idea he was the man that New York publishers referred to as Mr. Christmas.

Not once in all the years of Christmas stories and Christmas novels did anyone recognize Herb Allison, the author of the most acclaimed book of the last half-century, as the lighthearted bestseller of Christmas stories, Mr. Christmas.

Herb Allison had single-handedly kept the spirit of Christmas alive in America and other places around the world. He lived an incredibly happy life and no one knew. The five months he farmed each year were the part the locals knew, the seven other months he was a man they would never recognize.

The first page of his new book was life changing for many, it read in part.

"When one is young, disappointments are titanic and personal successes are often shallow and superficial. But with age, disappointments become opportunities and personal triumphs become less important, less meaningful."

The book explained his early life problems and his late in life successes. It was not about how to become rich and successful. Instead, it was about life's journey and it was what kept him going after his early disappointments. Christmas, it was Christmas, Christmas and the delightful season that kept him going. The season instilled his Christmas spirit of giving and sharing with others, and that kept him going. Christmas kept him from becoming an angry old man, instead turning him into both Mr. Christmas and the most influential writer of his generation

~14~
Homer Goes Home for Christmas

This one is for the kids.
Read it to the kids or grandkids.
Don't worry, it's still in the west, well sort off.

WARNING – *Story features a really cool Dragon.*

Homer had always wanted to go home for Christmas but never went. He wasn't sure why. He had not been home at any time of the year since he was a little one, and that had been, what, almost a 1,000 years. Sure didn't seem that long.

You see Homer was a dragon and dragons just don't go home, not often anyway. But now it was time and Homer knew it. Why? Because, in the entire world, there were only three dragons left, and all of them live in one kingdom, the Kingdom of Gniraw Lien or the GL as it was commonly called. Once there had been dragons all over both the known and unknown world, but no more. Just mom, dad and Homer, three dragons in all the world and they lived in the unknown world of the GL.

Homer was no ordinary dragon if there is such a thing as an ordinary dragon. Oh, of course, he could fly and breath fire, well, kind of. Breathing fire made him cough and he got altitude sickness, just a bit when he flew. Sometimes when he tried these extraordinary dragon powers he messed up, often really messed up.

A few years ago, couldn't have been all that long, maybe 150 or 160 years, anyway, not that long ago, Homer had thoughts, like he did this year, of going home for Christmas. He practiced singing a few Christmas Carols and tried to wrap a few packages. One day when he was out doing what dragons do each day, he happened by a magnificent Chestnut Tree. He loved singing, *The Christmas Song*, belting out the lyric, *"Chestnuts roasting on an open fire,"* with great gusto every chance he could. And that is where the trouble started.

When Homer did things without thinking, he often caused a near calamity. Chestnuts, beautiful Chestnuts hung all over a spectacular century old tree. At this time of the story, readers may have already guessed what happened next. Homer roasted the Chestnuts, roasted them with one mighty, fiery, coughing breath, roasted the

Chestnuts, tree trunk, branches, leaves, okay he caught the tree on fire. Homer got the heck out of there.

The GL was a great place to live. Homer had never known any other world and didn't want to. The GL was not huge, only about ten times larger than the earth, so not enormous, but large enough for Homer. Homer loved to roam and go about his dragonly ways. But he did have his job. It was his job to protect the GL treasury and to keep earth people away from the entry port into the GL. Now dragons, and there were only three, could move freely between the known earth and the GL but no one or nothing else. It was especially important to keep the people of the GL away from the earth. Management, that's what the government of the GL is called, didn't think that earth people would understand the citizens of the GL.

Citizens of earth and of the GL looked exactly the same and acted, for the most part, just the same. So why did Homer get paid to keep the people separated? Powers, the people of earth had powers that the GL citizens did not. Earthlings moved around by walking on two legs, the GLs could not do this. They had to stick to moving around by flying. The GLs could talk to each other but to do so needed to stand near them. This was not the case with the earth people who could talk to people many miles away. To do this, they simply held a tiny box to their mouth or ear and seemingly could talk to anyone, it was unbelievable. That is why Homer was paid to protect the people and he was a pretty good protector. In most cases, one look from the huge dragon did the job.

Management had become difficult of late, and Homer needed a break. Wanting to go home and see mom and dad, seemed like it would be a good way for Homer to relax. A relaxed dragon is an excellent dragon, Homer had often said. His mind was made up, he was going home. Christmas, well that was a bonus.

Homer packed a bag stuffing in a change of sneakers, his lucky hat, a few snacks, and a gift for mom and dad and he was off. Then he wasn't, he decided to grab a few extra gifts for neighborhood kids near his parents. But, Homer, being Homer, always over did it.

Now, he was off again, sort of. Homer ran over the rough terrain, stumbling and coughing and after a run of a bit over a half mile he was airborne. He flew the first few miles only six feet above the ground and twenty miles later he was finally able to reach his normal flying altitude of 83 feet.

Six hours, 21 minutes and a few odd seconds later, Homer reached his destination. He was home, in the far western part of the GL, the locals called it the Old West. Homer's dad was still the Marshall keeping gunslingers and other bad guys away. Homer crashed into the middle of Main Street, causing a spectacle and sending the locals racing for cover.

"Knew it was you, knew it soon as I heard you hit the ground." Homer's dad said. Then he reached out his front foot and helped Homer to his feet.

"Must have come home for Christmas, very thoughtful son but it's not going to be very merry around here this year."

Homer dusted himself off, smiled and said, "Gonna be better now, Homer's here." Then he coughed and started a nearby boardwalk on fire.

"What's the matter, why will there be no Merry Christmas here, I don't get it," Homer said.

"Well times have been tough this year not much money around, newsmen are callin' it a depression, or the start of one anyway." Homer's dad frowned and added, "But times have been tough before, next year will be better."

That short conversation ended the talk of Christmas for the day. Homer and his mom and dad spent a delightful Christmas Eve, reminiscing until past midnight after a superb evening meal.

Homer slept in the next morning, slept in until his mom hollered upstairs for him to get up, something magical had happened. Homer started down the stairs, tripped and tumbled down the last 40 or so. But he was fine, this was not the first time. He looked at his mother and said, "So what's this about magic, something magical happened?"

"Presents, every kid in town, every single one had presents this morning," She said.

"No one knows a thing, not where they came from or who brought them, Santa only delivers to earth, never in the GL." She stopped to take a breath and added, "Nothing has changed, not one thing, don't know how it happened, it's a miracle, a miracle for sure."

Then she noticed the hat, Homer had perched on top of his head, a bright red Santa hat. "You," she said.

A big smile crossed her face and she started to put her hands on her hips, then remembered she was a dragon and didn't have hands or hips. She dabbed a tear from her eye, coughed a small flame and said, "There is something different here, you came to town."

Homer was not sure what to say or what to admit, so he smiled and walked outside to enjoy the softly falling snow, a white Christmas.

"You better watch out
You better not run
Santa Dragon is coming to town
That's what I'm tellin' you now."

Homer belted out the lyric, even if it was only somewhat like the original. Ten minutes later, Homer, after a quick, "See you soon," was gone.

For years, people talked about Homer Santa and the year of the Dragon Christmas - and all was well in the world – both the known and unknown.

"Somehow, not only for Christmas

but all the long year through,

The joy that you give to others

Is the joy that comes back to you.

And the more you spend in blessing

The poor and lonely and sad,

The more of your heart's possessing

Returns to you glad."

   -John Greenleaf Whittier-

May all of you be blessed and your hearts warmed this Christmas season.

Neil

Bonus

The first Chapter of Neil Waring's new historical fiction book, **Commitment**, available through booksellers and online everywhere.

Commitment - Chapter 1

If the young cowboy had but one wish, it would be to live. He would be thinking of nothing else.

However, it was then obvious, he did. He thought back one minute to his unfortunate attempt to force legendary lawman Blade Holmes to draw. It was likely the worst decision he'd ever made. If present conditions were not so grave, he might have laughed but instead his mind flashed scenes of his impending death. The cowpoke felt the cold from the barrel of the Colt pressed under his chin and shivered, but not from the cold.

From the bony tip of the cowpokes shoulder, blood had started a slow seep through his threadbare shirt. The blood tickled his skin where the pain was still bearable. No longer standing tall, he seemed to tilt slightly backward, frozen.

Afraid to move, even to take a much needed breath, his eyes bulged, his face became an artist's pallet of changing colors, from bright red to what now was a hopeless blue-grey. Still conscious, or so onlookers believed, he slumped against the bar, fighting to stay upright. With the help of the bar, he was motionless except for the ever so slight in and out of his chest. The cowboy's feeble breaths moved him so little that, to the untrained eye, he appeared more a poorly constructed cowboy manikin than a man under arrest. He didn't have many years on him but was old enough to know it might be best not to move, not even so that he could fall to the floor.

As for the celebrated lawman, he looked business-like and appeared relaxed holding the six-gun tight under the chin of the wobbly young cowboy.

The moment had been magical; Blade Holmes reacted so fast to the situation that time may not have moved. Years from now people would swear, actual clock ticking time, had been stopped. Blade Holmes, already a legend in the West, made the impossible happen, for a moment he'd stopped time. And for a moment one young cowboy likely wished he could go back in time, to a time before he'd handmade the unfortunate circumstance that lead to his present calamity.

The once tough talking cowboy Blade held against the bar now looked even younger than his nineteen or twenty years, more a boy than a man. The beaten cowboy lowered his eyes, careful not to move any other part of his sweat-streaked face. His trembling right hand hung beside an empty holster. Bending forward, but only from the neck, he took in a long slow breath then focused both eyes on a grimy back smudge a few inches in front of the toes of his worn out boots.

The young cowpoke appeared afraid to look up, afraid if he did it might be for the last time. Betrayed by unsteady knees, he could no longer stand. His breathing changed to gasps; the young trail-hand looked like he might be sick. Onlookers, most now standing, backed off a step or two, waited for him to throw up, slump to the floor or both. The bars gambling clientele might have bet on how long it would take for one or the other to happen if there had been time.

Blade Holmes held the big Navy Colt with a steady hand, the butt of the gun pressing hard against the cowboy's breast bone the barrel wedged tight under his peach fuzz chin. The ongoing nervous state of the cowpuncher may have reached the extreme point several seconds back. It should have been about then when the realization had come to him. He'd not drawn his six-gun. There had been no time to touch his holster or gun.

To the young cowboy, everything in the barroom stopped when he went for his gun. However, time must have moved, maybe a fraction of a second passed, but not enough time for him to touch his right hand holstered forty-five. The wannabe gunfighter now looked timid, swallowing over and over, with his chest heaving, he licked his lips and then again, he looked to be only moments away from running or dying.

The tense situation eased and Blade's mouth curled into an uneven smile. He knew nothing more would happen, not today. Blade relaxed his grip, and the young cowboy slumped to his knees then stood back up and grabbed the edge of the bar with both hands. Raindrops of sweat ran down his face, dripped from his chin and speckling the front of his shirt. Blood widened the crimson spot around the newest hole in his soiled shirt. His face brightened and flushed with embarrassment as he stood fighting back fear, tears, acute nervousness, and worst of all, thoughts of dying.

Now an epiphany reached the young would be gun hand. His empty holster could only mean one thing. The gun under his chin, before he fell to the floor, belonged to him, not the sheriff, it was his gun. His mind produced a blurry picture of what must have happened. The thought took his breath away, he gagged, puked down the front of his shirt and on the chair beside him, and felt no better at all.

The shuddering cowboys mind started to clear, much too late. He realized the man he had challenged to draw, a man he did not recognize, was not just another small cowtown sheriff. The man he challenged was a mythological figure in the American West, the greatest, lawman, gunfighter, tracker and army scout in history. People wrote books about him, a man seemingly everyone but he knew all about.

The cowboy's shaking now became uncontrollable, his knees buckled and he started to go down, again. This time Blade caught him in the middle of a slow-motion collapse, laid the kids six-gun on the bar and grabbed his belt and elbow keeping him upright.

Blade Holmes had shot him, only a shoulder nick to stop him, and then had taken two steps pulled the cow punchers gun and pinned him to the bar, in how much time? Maybe, but the blink of an eye.

Blade relaxed his hold as the young cowboy started to come around, regaining some of his equilibrium, he took one small shuffling step back away from the bar. Paused, trying to take a deep breath, but instead gulped at the air setting off a coughing fit, hoping all the time his next breath would not be his last. A little braver now, he took a long blind backward step, caught a chair leg with the heel of his boot and toppled over. Hitting the floor with a groaning thud he rolled to his hands and knees, crawled a few feet, grabbed an empty chair and pulled himself to his feet. Looking around he thought for the first second in the past thirty, he might live.

His hat lay on the floor inches from where he stood. Bending straight legged from the waist, all the time his eyes set on Blade, like the quarry watching the hunter. He waited for something to happen and prayed nothing would. Scooping up the trail worn hat he adjusted the feather in the band, straightened the brim, and then placed it on his head as if this might be his last living task.

Moving as fast as he could, without running, he straight-armed the batwing doors and stumbled outside. Taking in as much of the dust filled fresh air as one breath would allow, he took a long step, hitched up his pants and yanked the battered black hat down to his ears. Stepping down from the boardwalk he stumbled, tried to run, but settled for walking, walking as fast as he could, away from the bar, and out of the life of Sheriff Blade Holmes, forever.

Within a minute of the young cowhands exit from the bar the patrons started moving again, most through the doors and away from the scene of the thirty-second altercation. Many had expected a shooting or at least a decent brawl, but Blade seemed to have a way of making this small prairie cow town more peaceful, much quieter, since his arrival in town a few weeks back.

The stories preceded Blade, stories about how quick he was with a gun and how good he could be with a knife. The stories seemed to be nothing but tall tales, bigger than life because, until today, no one had seen him in action. No others had tried him, all the rest, and there were a half dozen or so, backed down knowing Blade's reputation. The young cowboy, likely riding hard, minus his gun, and probably still shaking, had been the first to try Blade since he started Sheriffing in the small Kansas cow town.

Sheriff Blade Holmes had not only drawn his gun. In what seemed to be one fluid movement, one moment when time stood still, nicked the young cowpuncher, holstered his Colt, pulled the punchers gun and held it under his chin.

Three minutes after the young cowboy left town the bartender, Blade, and an old timer drinking coffee were the only ones left in the bar. The familiar stench of stale beer, cheap tobacco, and untidy customers hung heavy in the air. But the usual commotion, sights, and sounds of the bar had vanished with the customers.

Blade turned, scanned the room and noticed the old man in a rumpled black suit for the first time. Catching Blades eye, a knowing smile bending his weather-beaten face, he raised his cup in salute. Blade noticed the clerical collar, wondered momentarily why a parson would be in the bar, then nodded and turned back around. Almost as an afterthought Blade turned again, the old man, despite his age, seemed to beam as he sat at the corner table with his head down both hands wrapped around his coffee cup.

Blade Holmes stood tall at the bar, relaxed as if he'd only now awakened from a pleasant afternoon nap. The bartender did not look comfortable, instead he looked like a man in shock, or maybe it was disbelief. He stood nervously patting droplets of sweat from his forehead relieved the fight, or near fight, was over

It started like it always did in small towns along the trail. Confrontations like this were a way of life in the Kansas rail and cow towns Blade frequented for most of the past few years. The cowboy, a young man who might have been on his first trip up the Chisholm Trail, only a few months removed from life with ma and pa. The boy, eager to impress, and maybe prove something about his manhood had drawled. "Draw your Colt if you have the nerve, sheriff."

The young cowboy, who may have fancied himself a gunfighter, had likely never been anywhere before and never heard of Blade Holmes. A cowboy trailing cattle because it was all he could do or wanted to do. It had not been about anything, a young man feeling too brave or feeling too many drinks under his belt and trying to show the sheriff he was the better man. But he was not, not even close.

Blade supposed in another place and in another circumstance the young cowboy's bravado might have backed the law off, but today it could have got him killed. Blade Holmes never backed down, not part of his nature.

The young cowhand committed a simple mistake, a young man's mistake, and Blade recognized it for what it was. When possible, Blade liked to end things in a hurry without serious harm to anyone. The one sided duel following the deputy sheriff being called out may have been an embarrassment to the cowhand, but it left him alive and in reasonable health. In a few years, he might make up an amusing little story about the day he met Blade Holmes. However, for now, and in the near future, he could always blame it on too much to drink, go back to the herd and forget about it.

Blade laid his Kansas-dusty hat on the bar, changed his mind, took it back and sat it on the stool beside him, crown up. He reached both arms behind his back and stretched, then stepped his own version of a worn out boot up on the wooden bar-rail and asked for a cup of coffee.

The bartender squinted at Blade forced a wry smile, took the grimy dish towel from his shoulder and patted beads of sweat from his forehead, again. Turning to face the pot belly stove behind the bar he reached an unsteady hand for the ancient looking coffee pot. His senses returned quick enough, and he pulled his hand back wrapping it in his sweat dampened towel before taking the pot off the stove. Fumbling a chipped gray cup from under the bar he spilled a cup of coffee into it. A small stream of the thick coffee missed the cup, pooled on the bar, crept across and dripped to the floor. The bar-keep watched the black liquid move along the bar top then pushed the steaming cup through it toward Blade. He forced his second smile in the past half-minute and stared at the sheriff, now with a renewed respect and more than a bit of awe.

"Dang sheriff, you sure know how to clear a room, gonna have to quit yer scarin' my customers away, that's the first time since you got hired you emptied this place, the other times you just looked at em and trouble took off."

Blade sipped at his coffee like a man without a care in the world. The bartender stepped back blotted his forehead and turned pretending to rearrange the back bar.

"Didn't mean to, out of the office making my afternoon rounds, don't know what it is about this star, but it sure seems to bring out the worst in those punchers," Blade said, tugging his shirt loose trying to use the extra fold in a weak attempt to polish his badge.

"Especially the young guys," he continued, "think they need to call me out, try to scare me off." He sat his cup down, pinched his lips together and shook his head.

Blade blew across the cup, took a second small sip, frowned from the heat, sat the cup back down on the bar and gazed into it as if it were a crystal ball. Lost in thought, Blade continued to stare into the cup, looking like he was waiting for an answer from the dark liquid. But his thoughts had nothing to do with the now completed altercation or with the cup of scorched coffee he moved from right to left hand. His mind wandered much farther away than the cup sitting on the worn bar top or of the nameless cowboy riding back to the herd. His thoughts were of other places and other times, better times, things he should have said or done.

He fought the melancholy.

The bartender faked a smile, his back still to Blade, took the damp towel away from his face and patted his chest as if fighting off an impending heart attack. For a moment, he looked a bit like he'd been the one Blade had held a gun on.

He turned, adjusted the tall stool behind the bar and took a seat across from Blade. "Don't worry about it, you might a saved me a peck a trouble, scares me when I have to drag the double barrel out and run Cowboys out of here. Since you been here, I haven't needed to do it, no, not a single time. When it used to happen I would worry, stay up all night sometimes, thinking they'd come back after me, plus it tain't no good for business, no good a-tull. I'm glad it's my side you're working on.

How'd you do it, take away the kids Colt so fast and move so quick, makes me cat nervous and I'm only thinkin' about it?"

"Don't know, guess I always could," Blade answered, taking a third sip of coffee and frowning.

"I heard stories about you being fast, but you drew your gun and you drew that cowboy's gun, and he didn't have time to move. Not sure he even took a breath or had time to blink, don't think I wanna see you draw against someone in earnest, glad you're on my side. Still don't see how you did it, how anyone could move so fast – be so quick. Heard tell you was faster than the mornin' light itself now seems like weren't no exaggeration at all. Might not of even told the real story, I've seen the rays of the morning sun coming down a might slower than your gun, no sir, no exaggeration at all."

The bartender patted at his chest again, made a mental note that he was still alive and went back to mopping his forehead, then as an afterthought, ran the grimy towel over the coffee spill and tossed it toward the storeroom door. Leaning back on the stool he took a new towel from the back bar and alternated patting his face and keeping his heart beating with the marginally cleaner towel. Tiring to relax he locked his eyes in a stare, watching Blade drink his coffee, black, no sugar, and no cream, black.

Blade took a last sip from his coffee cup, stepped his boot down off the bar rail, dropped a nickel on the bar for the coffee, tipped his hat to the bartender, turned and walked toward the door. Pushing open the batwings he held them open for the stooped elderly man dressed in preacher's garb. Before letting the doors swing shut Blade stopped, looked back and said to the bartender, "Practice, used to practice some back in my younger days." Blade turned to say something to the old man, but the rumpled preacher was gone.

The bartender stood wiping at a few imaginary spots from the bar top waved a fistful of towel toward Blade shook his head and slapped the towel over his shoulder not knowing this would be the last he would ever see of Sheriff Blade Holmes.

Early the next morning, without a word to anyone, Blade unpinned his star, wiped it on his shirt, laid it on top of his letter of resignation and placed it on his sheriff's office desk. He walked the two blocks to the livery stable, saddled his horse and rode north.

Three weeks later, wearing the best suit of clothes he owned, Blade sat with his back to the wall playing stud poker on the third floor of the Cheyenne Club on Seventeenth Street in downtown Cheyenne, Wyoming Territory.

Commitment - Order your copy today, available as an eBook or in softcover.

About the Author

Neil Waring, born in O'Neill, Nebraska and raised in Fairbury, Nebraska was educated at Peru State College, Wayne State College and the University of Wyoming. He spent 42 years in education, teaching, American History, Wyoming History, and Geography along with a variety of other social science and English classes. Although the majority of his career was spent teaching at the high school level, he also taught Wyoming History, as an adjunct professor, for area community colleges for twenty years.

In addition to this book Mr. Waring has published a nonfiction book about the Civilian Conservation Corps and the building of Guernsey State Park. Also to his credit are two young readers, growing up books, and a western fiction novel.

Neil has also published multiple short stories and historical pieces both online and in print. He writes several blogs, including a popular Wyoming blog, Wyoming Fact and Fiction, at **http://wyoming-fact-andfiction.blogspot.com**

Neil can also be followed on Twitter **@wyohistoryguy**.

Neil and his wife Jan live in Guernsey, Wyoming near Fort Laramie, the Oregon Trail, the North Platte River, and beautiful Guernsey State Park. When not writing Mr. Waring spends time, taking photos, reading, gardening, playing golf, fishing, traveling and hiking in beautiful Guernsey State Park.

-Other Books by Neil Waring-

~ *The CCC & the Building of Guernsey State Park - With Folktales of the Park*   (nonfiction)

~ *Melvin, The E Street Ghost*   (young reader)

~ *Then Mike Said, "There's a Zombie in My Basement*   (young reader)

~ *Commitment* (Western Historical/Mystery)

All of Neil's titles are available as softcover books or in eBook format and can be found at all major online and brick and mortar bookselling sites, in Wyoming and nationwide.

Want to order online? Type, Neil A. Waring, into your favorite online bookstore site. He will be there!

Books are also available from the publishing site

http://oldtrailspublishing.blogspot.com

*Like a signed copy?

All books purchased from Neil's publishing site will be autographed. If a reader has bought elsewhere and would like a free autographed bookmarker, make a request through the old trails publishing site, any of Neil's blogs, or on Twitter **@wyohistoryguy**, and one will be promptly sent.

Neil Taking a Break in Wyoming's Guernsey State Park

67622707R00104

Made in the USA
Charleston, SC
17 February 2017